Uncle Mike,

A FINE LINE

By Alison Sky Richards

Enjoy the adventure!

Alison

10/7/17

Mike

Enjoy the adventure!

[signature]

12/2/19

Dedication

This tale is dedicated to the four men in my life

who will forever be brothers to me

Joshua Bradley

Robb Zahm

Paschal Frisina III

And

Joseph Gearhart

Acknowledgements

While there are many people who deserve appreciation for putting up with me through this process, there are a few who need to get special nods for their help – both by choice and some not realizing what they were contributing to.

First I need to thank two of my best friends – Emily Proulx and Bethany Kesler - who helped served as beta readers to make sure that this finished product resembled an actual story and not just a bunch of words floating around on a screen.

Continued thanks goes to the members of the Maryland Renaissance Festival's Fight School – Casey, Jim, Mike, and Geoff – for their fun and educational scenes that helped bring in some of the more colorful forms of dialogue in a fight than I thought I could do. They also introduced me to my S.A.F.D. instructor, Robb Hunter, who with him and his TA Craig Lawrence, I was able to learn how to use the weapon that I would eventually have as the focal piece in this tale to make this – as well as fight scenes in my many novels to come – well choreographed and realistic.

And finally, to the two men who I will forever be indebted to: Michael Stackpole and Aaron Allston. Years of on and off mentoring in exchange for minion services every DragonCon will shape my writing forever, and there is no amount of thanks that I can bestow to show my true appreciation. If it wasn't for their guidance, I would not have the courage or the confidence to be able to share my writing with the world. Thank you both for taking me under your wing, and I hope that I will continue to make you proud.

- *Alison Sky Richards, August 2013*

Chapter 1

Every heroic tale has a beginning. That said, sometimes that hero has to be brave enough to admit that his beginning may not be the most beautiful, the most charming, or even the cleanest one that has been recorded in all of history.

Such is the tale of Herrick Raffin.

The young man lay face down in the mud a moment before he slowly pushed himself up enough to look at the redheaded woman who stood over him, clutching a basket full of wild berries. Her hair was flowing wildly in the breeze that went from the forest down the hill and into the valley, a flowing fire that matched the anger in her eyes. "And if you *ever* try that again, your jaw won't be the first thing I aim for!" With her threat hanging heavy in the air, she picked up her skirts and stalked off towards the village that was just in the distance.

When she was gone, Herrick sat up the rest of the way and worked his jaw around to make certain it was still attached. There was a hint of a smirk on his aching lips. "I know you want me!" he shouted after her, but she didn't turn back or act as if she heard him.

As he stood, he noticed that his tunic and pants were completely coated with mud that was now starting to dry as the sun came back out and hit him through the spaces between the trees. He cursed softly, trying to brush it off with no luck. *I guess I won't have any clean clothes until I get some money or find a river*, he thought as he gave up and reached for his satchel.

At least that was still clean.

It was a short walk down the hill to the small farmer's village that only a few maps knew the name of - Barden. There was nothing distinctive to it; the Land of Mora was filled with tiny villages like this where farmers gathered to live far from the big cities. On his travels, Herrick had made his way through many of them and they were always the same.

This village, however, was filled with people looking at him and laughing at his mud covered appearance. Herrick tried to ignore them as he looked around, part of him wondering if none of them had ever seen a dirty person before.

His main purpose right now involved finding a job. For the past few days as he traveled from town to town, but every place he walked into immediately told him that they weren't hiring and kicked him out. His money was running low, and while he was a gypsy in spirit, he refused to just take what he needed. He would work for his food and a place to sleep, even if that was all he got for his day's labor.

As he reached the edge of this village, he found a place that he hoped could solve his problems. Taking a deep breath, he walked through the double doors of the Open Trough Inn. The second he entered he realized that the name of the inn suited itself well.

Directly inside the door was the inn's eating area. All seven tables were filled with men whose clothing was as dirty as Herrick's; only they didn't seem to mind their appearances. Each man had the look of a hard worker who was living just on the inside edge of the law.

A large, burley man with long red hair stood up to block Herrick's path as he started for the back. "Where do you think you're going, little man?"

Herrick chuckled, as he was by no means a "little man". He was taller than most men, but his slim, muscular build was nothing in comparison to the burley man's beer belly and arms as thick as a tree. "I'm looking for a place to work, or else just a spot in the kitchen to sleep for a night so I can move on tomorrow."

The man looked him over, taking in Herrick's muddy clothes. "How'd you get that filthy? Sleeping in a hog's pen?" Laughter from the man's table joined the rest of the inn.

"Actually I met up with a wild beast just outside of the village and had to do a little mudslinging."

The man gave him a glance, and then burst out laughing. "I think you'll work out just fine, lad." He held his arm out. "Name's Cairan. Last three lads who've tried to get a job have wet themselves under my little interview. You have a good backbone there, so you get the job."

"What kind of job are you looking to fill?"

"Whatever I find for you to do: errands, cutting firewood, cleaning up after hours. You still want it?"

Nodding, Herrick shook his hand. "Yes, sir."

"Then you start now. Lunch's almost over and Vesa will need help in the kitchen." Cairan pointed towards a door at the far-most right corner of the room.

"Is there a chance that I can clean myself up first?"

Cairan laughed his hearty laugh again. "I suggest you do. Get a set of kitchen clothes and there's a bucket of rainwater just outside the back door. Any other questions, ask Vesa."

Herrick grabbed his bag and started for the door. As he swung it inwards, he felt it connect with a person on the other side. "Son of a goat!" a female voice exclaimed as the sound of something hitting the floor echoed in the main room.

"I'm sorry!" Herrick said as he grabbed the door and opened it in the opposite direction, planning on helping the woman on the other side. Then he saw her and stopped.

"What are you doing here?" the redheaded woman from the path asked, glaring up at him.

He couldn't help but smirk back at her glare, even as he felt his jaw as it remembered the pain she had inflicted earlier. "I just got a job here. You must be Vesa."

The woman lifted her chin, letting the long red hair fall back from her hardened face. "Yes, I am, and my father owns this place."

Herrick felt Cairan appear behind them, and watched as he saw the look Vesa was giving the younger man. "Wild beast, huh?" Before Herrick could explain, Cairan held up a hand. "Go get washed up and get to work, lad. Every minute counts in this place."

"Yes, sir." Herrick grabbed the clean pants and

tunic from the pile near the door and ran outside to wash up, not risking the loss of his new job on an argument. When he was gone, Vesa turned to look at her father with those same hard eyes, but he just smiled and walked back out to be with his friends.

Chapter 2

Grace and skill come only after years of experience and practice. The young can only watch their elders in the hope to gain the knowledge that they wish to possess. Once they gain it, though, arrogance is sure to follow.

Such is the story of Master Price ord'Vanele.

"Come down from there, you little thief!" At the base of the tree stood a blacksmith, his arm held up in outrage while wielding a poker at the cloaked figure above him.

"I am not a thief; I have only taken what is owed me." Price looked down from the tree limb he was currently relaxing on. There was no fear in him at the man below. "You charged me double on the shoe repairs for my horse, and then not three hours away from here the shoe came off and my horse's leg broke. He was in so much pain that I was forced to end his suffering. I'm out a horse now, all due to your negligence." Finished with his reasoning, he crossed his arms and leaned back against the tree.

The blacksmith, however, was not satisfied. "You're blaming me for the death of your horse? That beast was older than me! I was amazed it was still able to walk when you brought it in. You should have destroyed it a long time ago."

Price glared down at the blacksmith. "That was my father's horse."

"All the more reason. Your father was a dissenter - he should have been strung up the moment he decided to join with the elves instead of killing them. Then our village wouldn't have to put up with his thieving half-breed bastard of a child."

The calm exterior of the half-elf broke, and with a cry of outrage, Price leapt down from the tree and tackled the larger blacksmith. The poker fell from his hand and landed a few feet away. Without giving the blacksmith a chance to regain himself, Price started to strike the man first in his stomach, then face.

It didn't take long though for the blacksmith to get his bearings and use his height and girth to his advantage. His thick hand wrapped around the neck of the smaller half-elf and picked him up easily. The man then slammed Price into the trunk of the tree a few times until Price stopped struggling against him and just hung limp. "Now give me back my money and if you beg nicely, I'll even let you go."

Narrowing his eyes, Price locked them with the blacksmith. "Never," he said in a calm, controlled voice. "You have wronged me, so I took what is rightfully mine, and nothing more."

"What you rightfully deserve is a royal beating…"

The blacksmith cocked his free arm back to strike Price again when suddenly his entire body froze in place. The only thing able to move was his eyes; ones that looked around in growing panic as the man realized he was trapped inside of his own frozen body. The eyes then turned back to Price, and the half-elf had a satisfied smirk on his face.

Gently, Price removed the blacksmith's hand from around his neck, finger by finger, and in particular removed them from the blood red pendant that hung from a gold chain around his neck. He then took his time as he adjusted his shirt and flicked a few pieces of bark from his cloak before he started to pace around the frozen man.

"I believe you are mistaken. No one 'deserves' a beating, no matter how much they 'ask' for it. The only thing *I* have ever *asked* for was to be treated fairly among this village." He turned away from the blacksmith to look at the town beyond them.

Elsieke was one of the major towns in the Land of Mora, and at one time had been a focal trading point between the elves of the hills and the human farmers of the valley. Price had lived there most his life; first with his parents until they left the city for another, and then his grandparents after their deaths sent him back. He had watched it nearly fall to ruins during the Great War, and saw it rebuilt into what it was now: a town that was a merchant's delight, but also one that no longer acknowledged the elves as their friends.

"But it seems that this place does not welcome me anymore." He looked back at the blacksmith, all emotion gone from his face. "Your words and actions today have made that perfectly clear."

The blacksmith stumbled backwards as Price touched his pendant and released the man from the spell he had been put under. He glared at Price and backed up towards the safety of town. "You're evil, just like your mother. If you ever step foot into this town again, I will see to it personally that you are strung up at the gallows and left there to rot."

Price laughed at his retreating form. "I would love to see you try." He stared at the distant town a moment longer, then turned and started to walk towards the bordering forest, lost in his own thoughts. After a few minutes he stopped, not looking up but instead closing his eyes. "So, do you approve?" he asked the individual who had appeared behind him.

"Somewhat. You let him live."

Price sighed and turned to face Zantos, who sat on a rock a few feet away. Master Zantos ord'Jan was the current leader of the Order; once a community in which human and elf lived in peaceful coexistence. All that was left after the Great War, however, were a small group of magic wielding elves. Price's parents, Evans Dalen and Selene ord'Nay, had formed the group before Price was even conceived as a community to show others that humans and elves could coexist, and it had helped heal a lot of hurt between the two species for decades. This was until those who lived in the cities beyond had deemed their efforts to be treason to the land and had ordered for their community to be destroyed.

The Great War had been a sudden and deadly battle. The human warriors came through their village just beyond Elsieke's borders without a care and attacked without mercy. The war didn't end until the remaining elves retreated far from the area, and it claimed the lives of nearly a hundred souls, including those of Price's parents.

Zantos graciously stepped into their position until such time that Price would be old enough to take on the role himself, but the Great War had forever destroyed the bond between the humans and elves.

No human dared to trust the elves in all of Mora now, and the remaining members of the Order were still angry at the actions taken against them nearly forty years ago – a short time for the lifespan of an elf. Price had learned through the years that this bond was broken on both sides - each with their own reasoning - and his childhood ideals to heal that rift were slowly fading away like the memories of his parents.

"The man did nothing to warrant death," Price stated.

"Yet he was going to kill you without remorse. He may still do so one day if you ever return."

"The ignorant are afraid of what they don't know or understand."

"You stole from the human. He understood that quite well." Zantos approached the young man. "Though you stated only took what you felt due and not a cent more." He *tsked* with his tongue as he fingered the pendant around Price's neck. "Where has my training gone wrong on you, Master Price?"

"I took what was owed. If I took more than that, then I would have been the thief he stated I was. I am not, as my actions showed."

"And where have you suddenly developed these human morals from, half-breed?"

Price hissed and pulled away from his teacher. "This group was formed on the love of a human man and an elven woman. My presence in life and in the Order is to remind you of that bond. We are better than that to ignore their values in our lives. All your lectures lately are of blood and murder."

The slap that fell across his face was unexpected, and a welt of blood rose up from where Zantos' fingernail had scratched Price's cheek. "The Order has changed, young Master, and you should have sense enough to see that. You will never be accepted fully as the Master of this Order if you do not follow our new ways."

Without another word, Zantos turned and started to walk deeper into the forest, expecting Price to follow him. Instead, Price stood his ground and didn't move or even reach up to wipe the blood off his face. "Then perhaps I no longer wish to be a member of this new Order."

Zantos spun back, surprise in his eyes. "Have you lost your focus on this?"

"No, I am tired of being something I am not, and yet everyone else believes me to be."

"And you believe that by leaving us you will find yourself?"

Price took a moment to reflect on that. It was true that he was the embodiment of the love between the humans and the elves, but Zantos had protected him in a time where the world wanted to kill him for being that reminder. Turning against the man would be like turning against his parents. "I don't know."

"You do know that if you choose to leave us, you will mark yourself for death. Once you are a member of this new Order, you are not allowed to leave."

"I understand that, Zantos, but I need to find a

purpose among you. So far, none has been presented to me that you approve of."

Zantos reached up to wipe the blood from Price's cheek, and then rubbed it thoughtfully between his fingers. "Then perhaps it is time for you to start taking your place among our cause. I shall speak with the council on this when we return to the keep. But for now let us depart. Darkness is falling, and we must not get in the way of the creatures of the night." He held his hand out, motioning for Price to continue walking, and they both disappeared into the shadows of the forest.

Chapter 3

It is a very well-known fact that the darkness of night is the best time to hunt, or to be hunted. Once the sun sets, a person walking on unmarked paths must watch for the dangers that the creatures of the night have set for the unwary and unprepared. Some dangers are obvious, like a sharp toothed bear charging down on you as they crash through the forest brush. Others are not, and even the most skilled of outdoorsmen can sometimes be ensnared in one of these more subtle traps.

Vesa stood outside the back door of the Open Trough with her arms crossed, waiting impatiently. The sun was starting to rise and Herrick had still not returned from his firewood gathering trip into the forest the night before. Chores still needed to be done before breakfast could be served, and she couldn't do it all on her own.

She hated to admit that she was worried. It had been a few weeks now since Herrick had started working at the inn, and she still hated him. Every time she turned around he was there; acting like the annoying, hormone driven male that she had seen that first moment they had met. So why was she worried about him now? For all she cared, he could have been eaten by some beast in the forest and she wouldn't miss him for a moment. Then he would be out of her life forever. She should be grateful to the beast.

But what if he's hurt, or in danger... he went to gather the firewood late last night only because I had asked...

There was a noise from behind the woodshed that made her turn around and grab the ax off the chopping block. "Who's there?" she called out.

No response came to her question. Instead she was able to make out some drunkard singing very off-key. A few seconds later, Herrick appeared around to side of the shed, holding a jug of ale that was broken on the bottom.

He was also naked except for the strings of a ripped cape that hung behind him.

Seeing her, his eyes lit up and he smiled. "Vesa, I killed a boar! It's out in the shed..." That was about all he was able to utter before he passed out, landing a few feet away from Vesa.

She stared at him a moment, then started to laugh as the shock finally wore off. First she put the ax back on the cutting block, then walked over and dragged Herrick to his feet. "Come on hero; let's get you sobered up before father wakes."

"*AH!* Ok, ok, I'm awake!"

Herrick ran his fingers through his drenched hair as Vesa stood beside him with a bucket that had contained cold water up until she had tossed it on him. "I was just having some fun. What's wrong with that?"

"Getting drunk and walking around the village

naked, then coming to work drunk and late… what else am I missing?"

Herrick smiled at Vesa scolded him. "You forgot about the boar."

"No I didn't; I'm looking at him." She tossed the rest of the water in the bucket on him before throwing it to the side. "And I'm telling father."

Jumping out of the tub he was in, Herrick grabbed her arm to stop her. "Vesa, please…"

"Let go of me!"

"Just let me explain, will you?" He did let her go though, instead reaching for the pants that were on a nearby chair. "I was gathering the firewood when I met up with a group of friends. I haven't seen them in forever, so we had a few drinks. I told them I needed to get back, and I was stupid and went back into the woods even though I couldn't see where I was going. I got lost, and then I ran into this… halfling. It had to be a halfling. Anyway, I asked him how to get back here and I told him I would lose everything I owned unless I got back. He said that he would take me back then if I gave him everything I owned."

"Which were your clothes?" Vesa raised her eyebrow, not believing the story at all.

"Yes! And I knew you'd hurt me more if I didn't show up, so I figured it was worth it. I gave him my clothes but he gave me this cape so I wouldn't get cold. We started back here and that's when we got attacked by this huge wild boar. I hit it over the head with the ale jug and I think it bashed in its skull or something."

"That is the worst lie you have ever told me, Herrick. I don't believe a word of it."

"I'm not lying, Vesa…"

"Just get dressed and get me the firewood you were supposed to find me last night."

"But Vesa…"

The back door burst open at that moment and Cairan walked into the room. "Herrick, my boy!" He was in a cheerful mood, and for some reason that put the young man on guard as Vesa glared at him.

"Yes, sir?"

"I saw the boar you brought back for supper tonight. Good work, lad!" The large man slapped Herrick hard on his back and then moved past them to head into the inn to start greeting the morning guests.

Vesa looked at him in shock, and Herrick just smiled in return as he walked out the back door to get the firewood.

Herrick worked hard all day to make up for his late start, and as the dinner rush ended, he was in the main hall washing the tables. This was the point of the night where Cairan and his friends gathered around the fireplace with some warm ale and traded stories from their times in the war. Some of the stories Herrick found hard to believe, but he couldn't help but listen into the tales the older men were talking about.

That evening, Cairan looked up and noticed the younger man listening in. When Herrick looked over again, he saw the large man wave him over to join them. "Jarak, tell the kid the tale of Tomli," Cairan ordered, looking at the old man who was sitting in the rocking chair with the pipe. "If he expects to be sticking around these parts for a while, he needs to know the story of this village's founder."

"The boy doesn't want to hear fairytale stories about ancient heroes," Jarak stated.

"Maybe not, but you will if you want another mug of ale."

Jarak laughed, coughing a moment on the smoke from his pipe before he relaxed back into the rocker's cushion. "You drive a hard bargain, Cairan. All right, where to begin…"

"The beginning is usually the best," Herrick said, putting his rag down and sitting on the edge of a bench.

"These kids, thinking they know how to tell a story? Boy, you never start at the beginning. Beginnings are boring and no one cares about the work a hero does on his path to greatness. It's that moment where the villain appears – now that's where a story should start."

Herrick rolled his eyes at the older man. "I stand corrected."

"Tomli was the first man to ever travel all of Mora in his life. At first, he went to just explore. Then, as he passed through places like ours, the villagers asked him to act as a judge over disputes. You see, a stranger is often the best judge of problems. He does not look at a problem with anything but his own heart. There are no influences from alliances and agendas. He is just himself, and to these people he was fair and honest.

"But at the same time, there was an evil demon that traveled the same trails, just a few steps behind Tomli. He would cause anger and discord among the people in the villages, and soon wars broke out over the same issues that Tomli had resolved.

"Years later Tomli walked the trails again to find the destruction in all these villages, and he asked '*How is it I left here in peace, and come back to find war?*' And in each village someone would say that a stranger came and showed the people greed and distrust.

"So one starless night Tomli waited in one of the villages, watching as the demon appeared and walked into an inn just like this. He sat among the people and listened to their stories and instead of trying to solve their problems, he fed into their fears and anger until everyone at the inn was shouting at each other.

"At that point Tomli stood up and shouted for the people to stop. '*Don't you see what the demon is doing? He is turning you against one another!*'

"The demon laughed at him. '*They don't need me to do that. I just help them along. Everyone feels anger. Everyone hates. You cannot stop that.*'

"The demon started to come after Tomli and they fought as the demon clawed at him and tried to find the anger and the hatred inside of him. But Tomli was a rare soul, as he had never hated a single thing. Even the demon, as he attacked, could not bring out that emotion. And that was when Tomli grabbed his sword and stabbed the demon through the heart, killing it.

"When the demon was gone, the people of all of the villages in Mora were released from the spell he had put them under. Tomli, however, had taken all the damage from the demon and was lying on the ground as his blood started to stain the earth. No one knew how to help him, but he held up his sword to one of the young men. '*There are demons like that in all of our hearts. Remember that when you think of me, and do your best to kill the demon before it destroys you.*"

Everyone was quiet as Jarak finished his story and took a sip of ale from his mug. Herrick had been listening intently the whole time, and finally spoke up. "Were you the boy that Tomli gave his sword to?"

"What?" Jarak nearly spat out his ale. "Boy, that's a story... a legend. You don't really believe it's true, do you?"

The other men in the inn started to laugh and Herrick felt his ears growing red as he stood up. "No, I guess not. Thanks for the story, but I should get back to work now."

He quickly grabbed the tray of dishes he had left on one of the tables and headed back to the kitchen. As he pushed the door open with his backside, he noticed that a familiar set of eyes backed away from the doorway moments before he opened it. As he entered the kitchen, however, Vesa was at the prep table, folding the dough to rise overnight for the morning bread.

She chuckled a bit as Herrick set the tray into the sink. "Don't feel bad. Jarak's been telling that story for years. I remember the first time I heard it. I was seven and even though he told me it wasn't real, I didn't want to believe him. My friends and I used to pretend we were big heroes and we would fight demons with sticks from the trees."

"I think we all did that as kids. Then we grow up."

"That we do." Vesa turned to watch him as he focused on the dishes. She hadn't found time to talk to him at length since the morning incident, and now it was almost as if she was seeing a different side of him.

"So, you weren't lying this morning, were you?"

Herrick turned to look at her as he wiped his hands dry. "About what?"

"The boar."

"Oh, that." Herrick tossed the cloth away and shrugged. "I don't blame you for not believing me. I was there and I still don't believe it."

"But how?"

"How what?"

"How did you...?" Vesa shook her head, laughing to herself. "Forget it. I don't want to know."

"Hey." Herrick grabbed her arm and turned her around to look at him. "Where are you going?"

"We've still got customers..."

"Cairan's with them, so they're fine." He tilted his head to look into her eyes and she quickly looked away. "What's going on here, Vesa?"

"Nothing."

It took a moment longer, and then a smirk came to his lips. "Oh, I see what's happening."

"What?" She turned back to look at him.

"You're starting to fall for me, aren't you? You're falling in love but you're trying to fight against it."

"I am *not* falling in love with you!" Vesa stated firmly as she pulled her arm free.

"So you're not?"

"I don't see how *anyone* could love you. You're arrogant... annoying... scruffy..."

Herrick just nodded as he walked closer towards her. Vesa, in return, kept backing up until she felt her back up against the wall. When she couldn't move any further, Herrick stepped in and cupped her cheeks with both hands before kissing her.

She struggled at first, but the gentleness of his kiss wasn't what she was expecting and soon she felt herself relaxing into it. Herrick felt her relax as well and smiled, deepening the kiss until he finally pulled back and smiled at her. "Now was that so bad?"

Vesa slowly wiped at her mouth, then smiled back at him before she slapped him hard across his face. Herrick stumbled back as he grabbed his cheek. "Damn it, must you always do that?"

"You just don't give up, do you?"

"I never give up when I want something bad enough."

She watched him a moment, then grabbed him by the shirt and pulled him back to her as this time she initiated the kiss. His eyes opened wide and after a moment he pulled away. "What was that for?"

"Because when *I* want something bad enough, I just take it."

"Then why did you slap me just now?"

Vesa smiled. "To remind you that I'm still the one in charge here, hero."

Herrick smiled, and there were no complaints as he wrapped his arms around Vesa's waist and they kissed again. He had finally gotten the one thing he had wanted since he had arrived in Barden, and life was finally starting to look good.

From the shadows of the woods just behind the

Open Trough Inn, two sets of eyes watched the interaction of the human lovers in the kitchen. Price had actually enjoyed the choreography of the exchange; watching as the man tried to best the woman, and yet it was the woman who truly held the power in this relationship.

Zantos snorted, not amused. "Humans are confusing, don't you agree?"

"I'm not confused," Price replied. "Women are very powerful in their race. Every heroic man has had a stronger woman behind them as their support. Men just have the assumption that they are the weaker race so they have a reason to protect them."

"I guess being part human yourself, you can understand them better than I ever could." Zantos laughed and then started to move around the side of the inn. "But we must not let this distract us from our business here."

Price followed closely in Zantos' wake as they walked to the front of the inn. There was a group of ten other elven men dressed in dark cloaks waiting in the shadows. Their hoods hid their faces, but each of them stood taller than the average man, and around each of their necks were various designs of a blood red pendant.

"What exactly *is* our business here?" Price asked.

"The same as always: hunting out the murderers of our brethren - of your parents. This man known as Cairan; he has their blood on his hands from the war. He may have forgotten those times, but we have not."

"The Order's memory lives forever," one of the cloaked figures spoke softly at Price's side. "And we avenge those who have fallen due to the hatred of others."

"This man spilt the blood of ours," Zantos spoke to

the group, summing up his strength and feeding it to the others in his words. "Now we will take *his* blood, as well as those who stand in our way, to pay for his crimes against the Order."

"Innocent souls do not need to die," Price stated. "This is only a debt that Cairan owes."

Zantos turned and scowled at the young half-breed. "Did the soldiers care about the innocents when they killed your parents? Did they not kill every man, woman and child in the village that was not hiding safely in the town beyond?"

He glared at Price until the young man looked away, and Zantos smirked before pulling his hood up. "And after all, they are only human."

Chapter 4

Vesa hummed to herself as she got back to work in the kitchen, thinking about Herrick who was now outside chopping firewood. After they had finished kissing – something neither of them were too quick about ending - they had talked quietly about how to break the news to her father. Vesa was pretty sure Cairan already knew about the attraction between them as her father tended to have the annoying habit of knowing everything before she did. She just wanted to make sure that he wouldn't try to beat Herrick up on some fatherly principle.

The joyful noises from the other side of the kitchen door went suddenly silent, which made Vesa stop. She waited a moment to see if her father would walk in after seeing the last guest out. When he didn't enter, curiosity got the better of her and she walked to the kitchen door and opened it a crack to look into the other room.

The main room held about a dozen figures in dark cloaks. All but one hid their faces in their hoods, hands wrapped around glowing red pendants. The guests who had been sitting with her father barely moved – almost as if they were all frozen in place; everyone except her father who was being confronted by the large elf that had his hood down.

"How dare you barge in here like this?" Cairan asked as he looked at his friends and guests in shock. "Who are you? What have you done to them?"

"Are you Cairan the Torch; hero of the Human-Elven war in the westward kingdom?"

"That was a long time ago." Cairan paled at the words. "I was a different person then."

Vesa jumped as she felt a body press up against hers from behind, and turned her head to see Herrick there, looking into the room as well. "What's going on?" he asked.

"Lower your voice," she hissed, then turned back to watch the men in the main room. "And I don't know, but they want my father."

"You still go by that name; therefore you shall answer to the crimes of that name." From his robe the elf drew a long silver dagger and held it up for the larger human to see it. Cairan started to retreat back, but the other elves had moved behind him to block his way.

"Leave my father alone!" Vesa ran through the door, unable to watch any longer. Herrick made a grab for her, but she was too fast and across the room in the matter of moments. She was almost to her father's side when she stopped suddenly, frozen in place.

Zantos turned to look at Vesa, and after a moment the edges of his lips lifted into a smirk. "So this is your daughter? She is a very beautiful specimen. Perhaps I should allow her to witness the death of her father the way many of us did."

"Please, no..." Cairan's voice begged. "She has no part of this..."

"Now, she will."

"Let her be." Herrick came out from the kitchen holding a short sword in his hands. His eyes looked at each of the elves in the room before locking on Zantos. The numbers were even now in each elf that was holding a human frozen. It gave him an advantage he was hoping he could use.

"Ah, the lover; finally the picture is complete." Leaving Cairan and Vesa behind, he moved towards Herrick with his arms outstretched. "You want to fight with me for your woman, human? Then come at me."

Herrick raised his sword to attack, but as he took his first step forward, he felt a wire wrap tightly around his neck. He was still able to breathe, but the wire cut into his skin as he tried to move away from it. "Don't be a fool and drop your sword," a voice stated firmly from behind him.

Doing as he was told, Herrick dropped the weapon. He then fell to his knees in front of the elf as they were kicked out from behind. Zantos smirked and stood in front of Herrick, looking down as if his eyes were judging the soul in front of him. He then held up the dagger in front of Herrick's face so that the human could see the engraving on the weapon.

"I want you to remember this night, human. It is your memories that will make you into the man that you want to become."

With that, Zantos spun on his heel and tossed the dagger across the room. It landed deep in Cairan's chest, and the larger man stumbled back into the wall. His hands went up to the dagger to stop the blood that was starting to flow from the injury as he slowly slid to the ground from shock.

"Cairan!"

"Father!"

With the deed done, Zantos motioned for the other elves to leave. They started for the door, walking backwards with their hands still on their pendants. Zantos ignored Vesa as he walked by until she spat on the back of his neck. "You monster! You can't even fight your own battles except to pick on poor, defenseless old heroes and their friends."

Wiping the spit from his neck, Zantos studied it a moment before looking at the woman again. He looked her in the eye, and then smiled. "You have a very fiery tongue, woman. Don't force me to remove it."

"I'd like to see you try."

He laughed at that. "You might just provide me with some amusement." He turned to the one elf that still remained in the room, holding his pendant and facing Vesa. "She's coming with us. See to her."

The elf nodded and approached Vesa. She wasn't able to move away as he whispered a few words and touched the pendant to her forehead. She gave a small cry and then her eyes rolled back into her head as she collapsed into the elf's waiting arms.

"Leave her be! You don't need her!" Herrick resisted the urge to struggle against the wire around his neck, but he did manage to turn his head a bit to look at the man behind him holding it. He was surprised to see the face of a man that was half human, and not the graceful traits of a full blood elf. What was more surprising, though, was that the same look of shock at the turn of events was in the half-breed's eyes as he watched the elf take Vesa out the door.

Zantos turned his gaze to Herrick, then the man behind him. "This time, I expect you to fulfill your task," he stated before turning to walk past the still frozen humans in the room and out the door.

The half-elf looked down at Herrick and for a moment they just looked into each other's eyes. Gritting his teeth, the half-breed took one hand off the wire as he grabbed a mug from the table. Herrick felt the wire loosen and tried to move to attack him, but the mug landed soundly across the back of his head and pitched him forward to the floor. Questions filled his mind as the blackness fell over him, the largest wondering just why he was still alive.

"Why did you take her?"

Price stood before Zantos, his eyes burning with anger as he stopped the elder elf. He had stayed quiet as they had fled the village, knowing that the safety of the group meant they needed to get into the shadows first. But now that they were out of danger, he couldn't hold his tongue any longer. "She did nothing except try to defend her father!"

"Why did *you* not kill the man who tried to attack me?" Zantos looked at the young half-breed's angry face with his own anger. To him, now was not the time to relish in the past. It was a time to celebrate the victory of another vengeance returned. "You disobeyed a direct command."

"He would not have attacked you. He just wanted you to leave the woman alone."

"How do you know that? How do you know he didn't have a dagger hidden in his cloak?"

"He wasn't wearing a cloak."

Zantos growled at that. He knew that the human hadn't been wearing a cloak, but to him it was the point that mattered: Price should have been obedient to his elders, not letting his morals stray into the care of others. "You've grown soft."

"I was not raised to kill the innocent."

The other elves of the Order had now stopped and were watching Zantos and Price argue. Zantos felt their stares and knew he could not let Price overpower him in their presence. "When they killed your parents, did they care about who was innocent?"

"There were no innocents in that battle. My parents fought and they died; so goes the life of a soldier. They knew it was an option going into that battle, and they went anyway to protect the ones like me who they didn't want to grow up in this kind of hatred. I mourn their death just like everyone else, and believe in the vengeance to a point, but others do not need to suffer for the mistakes of the guilty. We are supposed to show that we are better than this."

The elves exchanged glances at each other, and then they all turned their attention to Zantos. The elder elf looked away from them, trying to find a way to reprimand Price so that they could continue on their way. "We will discuss this later," he said finally and made to leave.

"No, we will discuss this now." Price ran and stood in front of Zantos, preventing him from passing. "You have changes the ways of the Order and gone too far this time!"

Zantos gritted his teeth and slapped Price across the face with enough force to knock the half-elf to the ground. "You speak of things you do not understand. Now be quiet and let's return home."

Price raised a hand to touch his cheek, and as he pulled it back he found blood pooling up at the open wound. "I'm not a child, and I understand perfectly."

The other elves had now grown tired of the fighting and went to stand behind Zantos. "He is no longer one of us," one whispered into Zantos' ear. "Destroy him and be done with it."

"We cannot kill the Master's son."

"Price has the right to ask these questions.."

"…but now is not the right time."

"Stop it, all of you!" Zantos waved his hand in the air, making a slashing motion to silence the elves. They did instantly, and Zantos looked down at Price. "Is this what you wanted; bring doubts into the Order, your parents' order, Master Price ord'Vanele?" Zantos twisted the title, making it seem more of a curse than the honorific it was.

"Doubts only arise when there are problems within the structure." Price rose to his feet.

"And I know what the problem is." Zantos approached Price and grabbed his pendant, pulling it from the young man's neck. "I grow tired of your tainted thoughts. You are now an outcast from the Order."

A hushed exclamation of shock went through the group, and Price glared at Zantos. "You can't do that."

"You said yourself that doubts rise when there are problems within the structure. You are the one who raises the doubts; therefore *you* must be the problem. As the one who has been given the power by vote, I am in charge of keeping the Order free from such danger."

"Including the destruction of the heir to it?"

"If that is how it must be, it shall be."

"So will you kill me now too? You've already spilt my blood, so be done with it and carry my death with the others who you have judged." Price lifted his chin, exposing his neck to Zantos but continued to glare at him down the bridge of his nose.

Zantos pocketed Price's pendant. "It is not for me to do at this moment. My mission is to return the rest of us home safely. However, the next time I see you, I will not hesitate."

Zantos turned to face the other elves. "Price ord'Vanele, the half-breed, is now one of the outcasts. Tonight his life shall be spared out of respect for his lineage, but the next time he is seen, you are all ordered to kill him without hesitation. Now, let us return."

Without a look back, all the elves moved past Price, including the one still carrying the unconscious Vesa. None of them dared to look at him in fear of Zantos' wrath after such a proclamation.

Price watched them disappear, and then smirked as he brought his hand out from behind his back and looked at the blood red pendant that lay there. He carefully put it back around his neck, sent a silent thanks to the stars for his skills and sparing his life, and then walked back into the woods to plan his next course of action.

Chapter 5

Cold water thrown on his face woke Herrick out of his dreamless sleep. For a moment, he thought it was Vesa trying to sober him up again. Yet, when he opened his eyes, he was looking instead at the face of Lars, one of the local woodcutters.

Herrick jumped to his feet, and instantly regretted it as his legs swayed under him. Lars grabbed his arm, steadying him. "Thanks," Herrick said. When he got his balance, he looked around the room. "Where did they go?"

"They disappeared into the woods."

"Herrick!"

Herrick turned and saw Cairan lying on the ground in a large puddle of his own blood. The men who had been frozen in the inn were now kneeling around him, giving him whiskey and trying to stop the bleeding with the tablecloths. Herrick went and knelt beside the big man.

"They took Vesa." Cairan asked. His eyes were clouded and he didn't focus on anything in particular.

"I heard."

"You must get her back." Cairan tried to stand but he was weak and didn't make it more than a few inches off the ground. Herrick placed a hand on the big man's shoulder to keep him still. "She's all I have left, and she shouldn't have to pay for my mistakes."

"What mistakes?"

"A battle - one that never should have happened." Cairan's eyes drifted closed. "When you find Vesa... tell her I love her." And with that, the last breath Cairan would ever draw was released.

Herrick held back the tears that threatened to flow as he realized that all the eyes of the men were watching him. Setting a stern face, he turned to face them.

"Lars, go upstairs and find a proper outfit for Cairan to be buried in." The man nodded and left.

"You four work on digging a grave outside near the family plot for him."

"Someone needs to run to the stonecutter and get a headstone."

"... and you inform the villagers and any other family he might have."

After assigning all the jobs that he could think of, Herrick found himself alone with Cairan's body. He found he couldn't look at the dead man, so instead he started to pick up the overturned chairs and tables to make the place presentable again. When he was almost done, Lars returned with a soft tunic and pants, and a beautiful silk cape. "These were his favorites," Lars explained.

"They're perfect. Help me lift him onto the long table so we can dress him."

Lars and Herrick lifted Cairan, then stripped him of the bloody clothing and dressed him in the nice ones. When they were done, Lars turned to Herrick. "What are we going to do about the elves and Vesa?"

Herrick didn't answer. He was staring at the long silver dagger that lay on the ground where Cairan had died. He walked over to it and picked it up, wiping off the blood on the discarded shirt. "Leave that to me."

The funeral was short with only a few mourners. When Cairan had said that Vesa was all he had left, he had really meant it. There was no family left in their line except for his daughter to speak for the great man. *But I will get her back,* he thought to himself, *and we will continue on the bloodlines of both our dead end families.*

Herrick had returned to the Open Trough Inn to close it up for what could possibly be a long time. Everyone in town had agreed that Vesa would be the next owner of the inn, or Herrick if Vesa never returned. Since Herrick was the only one there, he opted to close the inn down until he returned, then give it back to Vesa.

He had just finished putting up the final chair when a stranger entered the inn, draped in a black cloak. "Sorry, Mister, but we're closed."

"I'm not looking for a room," a voice returned, one which made Herrick look up with hard eyes. He knew that voice. It had an elven tongue to it, and he didn't know any elves except…

The stranger pushed back his hood, revealing the half-elf who had held him with the garrote wire. "I'm looking for some help."

Herrick gritted his teeth and stared at Price. "The only help you'll find here is the path to your grave!"

Charging, Herrick tackled Price right into the wall,

the half-elf's head hitting backwards to stun him. Herrick then drew the silver dagger from his belt and held it at the other's throat. "Where's Vesa?"

"She is being taken back to the stronghold. I don't know the path they plan to take, but I can take you to where they are going."

Herrick held the dagger a little closer to Price's voice box, anger making his whole body shake. "You have three seconds to explain before I start cutting."

Price closed his eyes. "I have been cast out of the Order because I refused to kill you and objected to the taking of your woman. You want her and I want my family's Order restored. Both can be accomplished together… with the destruction of one elf."

Herrick locked eyes with the half-elf, looking for any signs of treason. "What kind of help do you want from me?"

"I can get in, talk to them, but I can't fight them. Not alone. The love you have for your woman will help you through the battle, and we will succeed. We have to."

"How do I know you aren't trying to make up for what you got tossed out for?"

Price looked down at the dagger. "You realize it is easier to talk without a blade pressed against your throat."

"It's also easier to fight when you don't have a wire wrapped around your neck," Herrick replied. "Until I make my decision, the dagger stays."

"Very well." Price took a deep breath and he felt the pressure of the dagger soften a bit. "I don't believe in killing innocents, and I considered you one when it came to the events of yesterday. If I didn't have this moral, that garrote would have sliced your head off the second you came through that door."

Herrick considered the words and then released Price but he did not put the dagger back into its hiding spot. "And what is your plan, elf?"

Price dusted off his clothing. "Half-elf. My father was human."

"You hang with elves, you're an elf." Herrick shrugged his shoulders and pulled down a chair to sit in. "You said you had a plan. You do have one, right?"

Price nodded. "We're going to need some supplies. It is a long journey. The stronghold is a good three day ride from here."

"That makes it a ten day walk. Through the west or south woods?"

"West."

Herrick whistled. He had walked through those woods on his way to the village all those months ago. He had been attacked multiple times and had almost become dinner to other creatures every step along the way. "You must be fools to live in those woods."

Price raised an eyebrow. "Who is more foolish: the one who lives in the woods, or the one who would try to seek the ones who live there?"

The two made plans for three hours in which Price indicated the supplies that they would need. "It would be faster with horses," Price indicated.

"There aren't any in this town I could even borrow. You're lucky I can barely afford to buy the amount of food we will need. A kitchen boy doesn't pay enough, and we buy things every day here so there is no supply cabinet I can reach into for things."

"I could borrow some for us."

Herrick laughed. "Right now, any elf who even walks into the village will be killed. Cairan was the best friend of everyone in the town. His death hurt many."

"Yet only a few showed to pay their respects."

"You were there?"

"I needed to find you, and I knew you would be there so I followed you back afterward."

"Did you pay respect to the life lost at your Order's actions?"

Price's body went stiff. "I have my own reasons not to pay respects to your friend, but I can acknowledge that his loss does hurt you."

With his hand, Herrick waved the thought away. "That we can discuss another time, elf."

"Half-elf."

"Whatever. How about I just call you Charlie?"

"My name is Price. Master Price ord'Vanele."

"Master?!" Herrick leaned back in his chair and laughed. "Master of what; protecting the innocent?"

Price stood up and gripped the table with both hands. "Are you going to continue mocking me or are we going to try and fix the things that were wronged yesterday?"

Herrick watched Price closely. "Alright, keep talking."

Price sat back down and looked at the sheet of paper in front of them. He has sketched a map of the woods leading to the Order's stronghold. "They should be here by now." He pointed at an area one third of the way through the forest. "I'm sure they have your woman on my horse, as so not to slow any of them down."

"Which means what?"

"It means that we will be in that spot at the time they are arriving at the stronghold. However, if I remember our path correctly, we can cut a day or even two off our journey by going through the old graveyard." He pointed to an area halfway through the woods. "Zantos does not want to ride through it, so they took the long way around it. The graveyard is fairly large and once you are in it, there is no turning back."

"I don't remember a graveyard in those woods." Herrick looked at the map. "Are you sure you're thinking of the same woods I am?"

Price nodded. "The graveyard is hard to find if you don't know where to go. The path has been long covered over with brush, but I know the way."

"As long as you know it. I don't like getting lost in the woods."

"We won't get lost. Now, we should rest. It's late, and the creatures of the night will start prowling soon. I really don't want to be seen as dinner tonight, do you?"

Herrick nodded. "I'm going to go into town and get the supplies then. I suggest you hide out in the barn until tomorrow. Don't let anyone see you."

Picking up his cloak, Price nodded. "You know, I never meant to even enter this battle. I tried to stop it before it happened."

Herrick was at the door, and he turned around to examine the half-elf. "What's done is done, and saying that won't make me think any better of you. We travel at dawn, half-elf."

"My name is Price."

Herrick did not answer, but instead went out the door and slammed it shut behind him. Alone in the inn, Price examined the place. It had been a long time since he had been in a human dwelling, ever since he had left his human grandparetns to take his place in the Order. Though a totally different person made it in a totally different village, the inn still had the same feel that his grandparents house had. It felt warm and welcoming. A shiver ran up his spine at the thought of the actions it had seen in the past day.

True, he did not mourn Cairan's death. After all, he had been one of the many who had a hand in killing his parents. Yet, the woman had not even been born when that had happened and neither had the man, Herrick. The fact that this place of welcome and warmth had turned into a place of terror for them was a sad thing, indeed.

With a final look around the room, Price made his way through the back door to the barn to sleep.

Chapter 6

Herrick woke early in the morning, before the sun had even started to rise. Wanting to get on the way of their journey, he quickly dressed and went downstairs to the main part of the inn. He stopped as he heard something and looked around, not needing any more surprises.

Then he heard it again. There was a faint knocking at the main door. Shaking his head, Herrick went to it and placed a hand on the handle. "We're closed," he told the visitor through the door.

"Herrick, I have something for you."

Herrick recognized the voice of the old storyteller, Jarak, and he opened the door. The old man was standing on the porch, leaning hard onto his cane while a package was wrapped under his other arm. "About time you got to the door. Man could catch his death of cold standing in the fog."

"I didn't know it was you, Jarak."

The old man scowled and pushed his way in, hobbling over to the first table and then giving Herrick a look. He quickly grabbed a chair down for him to sit in, and Jarak did, putting the package on the table. "I heard you were setting out to find Vesa. This will help you."

He pushed the package closer to Herrick, who opened it. Inside the wrapping was a sword. It was a light weight, one handed short sword with a gold hilt that curved around gracefully to protect the wielder's hand. "I can't accept this, Jarak."

"Boy, I don't have use for it anymore. It'll treat you well. Every hero needs a good sword after all. I've seen the old piece of steel you have, and this is a major improvement. At least it doesn't look like it'll break in battle."

"Thank you. I'll use it wisely."

Outside, the sun was starting to rise and burn away the fog. "I had better get going. A man needs to find a warm fire and a hearty breakfast." Jarak stood back up and stretched a bit, then looked at Herrick seriously. "I expect that to be here again soon. So take care, come home safe with Vesa, and leave none of those elves alive."

"I will." Herrick promised and he walked Jarak to the door and only closed it when the man was hobbling back down the path towards the main part of the village. When he turned back, he saw Price standing against the far corner of the room that the sun was not lighting up brightly just yet. His eyes were locked on the sword, then lifted to look at Herrick. "Let's go," he muttered and started for the back door.

Their first day of travel was uneventful. Price kept to himself, not speaking to Herrick unless it was absolutely necessary. The whole time, all he could do was stare at the sword that now hung on Herrick's hip. Herrick had said that he would use it wisely, and Price hoped he kept true to those words.

As night started to fall, Price stopped and looked around the woods, then up into the treetops. "This is as good of a place to stop as any," he stated, dropping his bag.

Herrick turned to face Price. "There is still another hour before true night. We can keep going."

"Night falls faster in the dense of these woods. Don't be fooled by what you see. It will be darker before you know it. We have to set up camp now."

"No, we travel more. Come on."

"I'm staying here. If you wish to continue, I will find you in the morning." With that, Price started to set up his camp. Herrick just shook his head and continued on.

Thirty minutes later, the forest was so dark that a person would be unable to see more than a few feet in front of them. Price sat by his fire, munching on a carrot when Herrick wandered in, out of breath. Price looked up at him and smirked, not saying anything.

Sighing, Herrick put his bag down and noticed that Price's pack was nowhere to be soon. "Where are your things?"

Price pointed up into the tree with his carrot. Herrick followed the direction and saw that Price's bag was hanging from a high branch, out of the grasp of anything that would be on the ground. "Why did you put it up there?"

"The food is safer out of reach of the wild beasts, do you not agree?"

"But if we need anything during the night, we have to climb up there to get it."

"That is why I plan to sleep in the tree as well."

Herrick raised an eyebrow. "Sleeping in the trees? Is this some kind of elf thing?"

"No. It is an 'I don't want to be eaten by some wild beast in the middle of the night' thing. Being in the trees means that they cannot reach me either."

"I thought we would set up watches."

"Then we would only get four hours of sleep each. Not a good way to travel. If there were more of us, then yes it is a wise choice. But not with only two."

Herrick looked up in the tree again. "I'm not sleeping up there."

Price stood and finished his carrot. "I am not surprised, but suit yourself. Sleep well." Price nodded his leave, and then quickly jumped up into the tree, climbing with long taught skill and grace until he got to a nice, thick branch and stretched out on it.

Herrick watched from below, amazed at how comfortable Price looked. He thought of himself trying to sleep on one of those branches and knew that somehow in the middle of the night, he would turn the wrong way and fall out of the tree and onto something. Shaking his head, he sat down by Price's fire and started to cook a strip of meat for himself before going to bed.

A few hours later, Herrick was still wide awake, afraid to sleep. His ears kept playing tricks on him. Every time he was about to fall asleep, something in the woods would move, rustle some bushes, or cry out and it would snap him back into alertness.

"This is ridiculous," Herrick muttered as he turned over in his sleeping roll. Glancing upwards, he could faintly make out Price sleeping peacefully above him. Sighing, he covered his head and tried to sleep again. *This is going to be a long trip, indeed.*

It was deep into the night when Herrick got his only warning. The fire had gone down to a glow and the shadows of the forest were covering the clearing. He heard the footsteps coming beside his sleeping roll, and was able to turn before finding the sword pressed against his chest. "Don't move," a voice ordered.

"If you're looking for money, I don't have any," Herrick responded. He had let his gaze follow up the path of the sword and peered into the shadows to make out the face of the person holding the weapon.

The being was a human male, about double Herrick's age with half the hair. His face was twisted, but Herrick wasn't sure if it was due to the shadows or its own deformity. "A young man in the woods with no money - that's a likely story."

"You think I would sleep in the woods if I had money?"

Another shadow came into the dying light. A similar man, but instead of the hair loss, he only had half of his teeth. In his hand was the sword that Jarak had given him before he had left the village. "This is a fine sword. Where'd you get it, boy?"

"It was a gift." Herrick looked over at the other man, but let his gaze move past him and into the trees where Price had been sleeping. Even though it was dark, Herrick could see the branches in the moonlight. His bag was there, but Price was nowhere to be seen. *Figures,*

Herrick thought, *the first sign of trouble and the half-breed disappears.*

"From your father, right?" The first man sneered. "A gallant knight who died in the elven wars, I suppose."

"It's a fine piece of work, that's for sure. Gold hilt and all. I think I'll just keep it."

The first man looked at the second, angry. "Hey, we're splitting this fifty-fifty. If you get the sword, what do I get?"

"Whatever else the boy has left."

Herrick listened to the two argue, then decided to make his move. As the first robber shifted to confront his partner more, he lifted the sword just off Herrick sternum. Using this, Herrick was able to slip out safely from under it, and then stood up behind the man. He tapped him on the shoulder, then swung his right fist around and into the robber's jaw.

The man dropped, and the second lifted the sword to go after Herrick. At that moment, a thin wire came around his wrist and forced him to spin around. Price continued to move, swinging the robber around further until he crashed into the tree.

By then, the first robber was back on his feet and he wiped the blood from his mouth. "You'll pay for that, boy." He came at Herrick, swinging his sword and forcing Herrick to dodge around the campfire. His eyes frantically searched for his other sword that had been used to cut more firewood. It was nowhere to be seen, and instead he grabbed one of the logs that hadn't been cut and held it up like a club.

The two men exchanged blows until a kick in the

robber's stomach forced him to drop his sword. Herrick took a swing with the club, but the man grabbed it and struggled with Herrick for control until the robber managed to pull it free from Herrick's hands and knocked Herrick onto his back with a hard swing at his stomach.

Something cold and sharp rubbed at Herrick's side as he landed and his hand wrapped around the handle of his other sword. As the robber swung again with the club, Herrick brought the sword up to block it, then worked to get to his knees and feet as the robber tried to push down against the weapon with all his weight.

On his feet, Herrick shifted his weight so that the sword and club went down harmlessly to the side, and he pulled back his arm to hit the robber in the face with the hilt of the sword. He dropped the club, and Herrick kicked out to make the robber fall to his knees. One final punch was all it took, and the robber fell to the ground, unconscious. Using the tree to keep his balance, Herrick took a deep breath and looked around the campsite. He needed to know where the other robber had gone with the gold sword.

"What took you so long?"

Herrick swung his sword behind him without thinking and Price managed to get out of range quickly. "Be careful where you swing that. I am not the enemy here."

Herrick snorted. "Where were you when they showed up?"

"Those two could not have been any louder. I heard them approaching half a mile away."

"Where's the other one?"

Price pointed over his shoulder. Herrick looked and saw the man in the shadows on the ground, his arms bound behind him. "You didn't kill him?"

"Neither did you."

Herrick looked at his opponent, who was still passed out. "True. We should move though before they wake up." He spied a money purse on the unconscious man and quickly bent down to retrieve it and hide it into his jacket.

"Agreed." Price jumped back up into the tree to retrieve his bag, and then landed next to Herrick. "You ready?"

Herrick quickly put his things back into his sleeping roll and rolled it up. He then looked around. "The other sword - where is it?"

Price looked around the camp with his elven sight, then spied is in the shadow of the tree he had swung the robber into. He pointed it out to Herrick and the human retrieved it. "Let's move."

Chapter 7

The two walked all day and into the next night before they set their camp, and then started again as the sun rose for their third day of traveling. Price noted with a smile when Herrick decided to join him in the trees after the previous night. *As long as we can learn to trust each other's advice,* he thought, *I know we shall survive this trip.*

They were now deep into the woods, and Price was relying on his feelings to guide them along the obscure paths. He had spent part of his childhood in these woods, and knew exactly where they were. The years had changed it though and now it felt different to him. It was colder.

"How much longer until we reach the graveyard?" Herrick asked.

"We are on the outskirts now," Price replied. "We should be there by late afternoon."

Herrick nodded, then stopped and looked up at the trees. "You know, we're really deep into these woods. Why would someone put a graveyard all the way out here, instead of near their village?"

Price worked to keep the pain that rose up from entering his voice, and instead took a deep breath. "You will understand when we reach it."

Herrick was surprised at the suddenly wave of emotions that rolled over the half-elf's face, but knew better than to ask the questions he wanted to. Instead, he just watched Price closer as they continued on.

A few hours later, they reached a clearing. The trees thinned out at the edges of the open area. From those trees hung strings with feathers and pipes that were used almost as if they were marking the territory. Price reached up and gently touched a certain formation of two pipes with a feather that hung between them. He stared at it a moment, then they both started into the clearing.

Herrick noticed that the graveyard was not a traditional one that humans had with headstones. There were no statues, no pyre or altar, and no markings at all to show where the resting place of the loved ones were.

Instead, Herrick found himself standing in the center of a burnt out village. The remains had not been touched by either beast or man. The wood that remained between the few stone walls showed that the fire had consumed the village a long time ago, and the footsteps that Price made in front of him were the first set of new tracks in what had to be years.

Price stood at the threshold of one house that was still standing. One of the stone walls had collapsed in, and the roof had long burned away with anything that might have been inside. He placed a hand on the stone entranceway as he closed his eyes and just let himself feel. Lost in his emotions, he didn't notice Herrick come up behind him.

"What is this place?" he asked softly.

Price turned to face the human, and Herrick could see that the half-elf was overcome with emotions he was trying not to display. "This… this was my home."

Herrick's eyes lifted to take in the place. "Your home?"

With a nod, Price turned back to look at the burnt shell. "Yes. I grew up in this house on the second floor… when there was a second floor. My mother and father loved it here. They helped bring the elves out of the woods to live with the humans. Our village was once intertwined with the trees before the fire destroyed them. We were far enough from the harbor town that the elves were willing to trust them. They started a community: The Order."

"The Order? The same group that attacked the inn?"

Price shook his head. "Yes, but no. We were not always apt for revenge. I do not expect you to believe me as I tell you." He looked at the empty town a moment, then the setting sun. "We may as well rest here the night."

"Here?" Herrick also looked over the town. It looked bad enough now, he wasn't sure he wanted to see what it looked like in the moonlight.

"It is actually safer than you would think," Price stated. "No one dares to walk the grounds at night as to disturb the spirits that reside here."

"And you feel we can sleep here just fine?"

Price walked through the archway and looked at the large room. "I did live here too. I do not think the spirits of my parents would object to me returning home one more time, and bringing a friend along."

Herrick sighed and followed him in. "I hope you're right, Price. I don't feel like getting into a fight again tonight."

As the moon rose to the center of the sky over the empty town, a fog started to roll. Eerie shadows fell across the center streets, cast from the remaining walls and trees.

Inside his home, Price stirred in his sleep. A ray of moonlight slipped between the cracks of the wall to illuminate his eyes and brought him out of his dreams.

He looked around and found that even with his ability to see in the dark, he had trouble seeing. The fog had gotten thick, but even it couldn't block the movement at the main archway as a shadow walked past. Quickly, Price grabbed his garrote wire from his pockets and wound it around his hands as he made to follow.

When he got closer to the archway, he saw a shimmering image in front of him: a human soldier staring out at the abandoned streets. Price could see right through the man, yet he knew that this was something more than an illusion. The face of the soldier was half-hidden by a helmet, but it couldn't stop Price from recognizing him. "Father?"

The soldier turned his head and saw Price. Seeing the strange face with pointed ears, the man's hand went to his sword. "Who are you?" he demanded.

"It is me, your son - Price." Stepping closer, the half-elf tried to search his father's face for a sign of recognition. "You are Master Evans Dalen, leader of the Order, are you not?"

"That I am. But my son is but a child. You are far too old to be him. You should be a soldier in my army."

"Father, it has been forty years. I have grown."

"If you are my son, prove it to me."

Price nodded, and he reached into his shirt to pull his amulet free. It was the only thing he could think of that his father would recognize.

It was an old tradition among the members of the Order. All the members, human and elf, had a special connection to nature which granted them unique powers. The parents would make an amulet from a mixture of their powers as a gift to their child on their fifth birthday. It was crafted to recognize the family bloodline so only they could use the power that was trapped within. Brothers and sisters would be able to band their power together since they were all the same. If anyone outside of the family line were to try and touch the jewel, the magic would overtake their body and paralyze them until the real owner returned to release them.

The ghost soldier examined the amulet, and then nodded. "That is of my blood," Evans stated, and then his eyes focused on Price as if he was seeing him again for the first time. "My son, has it been that long?"

"Yes, it has." Price found himself smiling – not a common habit of his. His parents had died in this battle when he was still a small child, and it was on that day he had forgotten how to feel happiness. "Where is mother?"

"She is over by the armory, preparing for the battle."

Evans touched Price's shoulder as he pointed across the street. With the touch, the fog in his vision cleared and the whole scene opened up in front of the young half-elf. He could see soldiers – elven and human alike – all in the robes of the Order and taking up hiding spots. His mother,

Selena ord'Nay, a beautiful silver-haired elf with violet eyes, was walking from spot to spot and making sure that each group had whatever food, weapons, and medical supplies they needed.

"What are you preparing for? This battle ended a long time ago."

"Not here," Evans stated as his eyes focused on a spot in the distance. "Every night we fight once more, and will not rest until the evil ones come back no more. See, there? They come." He pointed to the hills, and left Price's side then for the streets, shouting a warning cry for his soldiers to prepare for the incoming attack.

Price turned to look, and saw what looked like hundreds of men on horseback entering the town with their swords raised and their battle cries echoing off the walls. They wore mismatched armor, which meant that they were no more than a group of hired mercenaries that had been banded together for the cause of another.

They dismounted from their horses and started to attack the members of the Order. Swords clashed, striking ghostly armor or flesh. Many cried out in pain and fell to the ground, their ghosts falling to the death that their real bodies had suffered forty years ago.

Price saw his father rush across the battlefield, attacking the mercenaries as he tried to make his way to Selene. She stood behind a water trough, holding out her bow and shooting arrows at the men still on horses as they entered her area. They fell from their horses, letting the animals continue to run through the village without a rider.

A shadow appeared behind his mother, and before Price was able to scream a warning to her, a sword flashed through the moonlight and landed along her back. Selene's cries of pain were cut short as her body was kicked forward, and she landed face first into the already bloody ground. She did not move.

Evans noticed his fallen wife. "Selene!" he cried, pushing his way through the battle that was between them. The mercenary that stood over her turned and pointed the bloody sword at him, and Evans raised his sword in return and charged at the man. The two met together in a flash of light and their swords sparked with each blow.

Price pulled out his garrote wire and took off after them. Something in him told him it was his place to be at his father's side; perhaps if he was able to stop the mercenary from killing his father just this one time, maybe this ghostly war would end and his father would return. Using the wire, he was able to wrap it around the sword arms that attacked him and twisted away. A few hands were severed as he pushed past mercenaries, but he did not let any harm come to the members of the Order.

Then there was another flash of light, and Price looked up to see his father gripping his chest. The mercenary stood above him, holding his sword's hilt as it dug under the ridge of the armor and into Evans.

"No!" Price's scream echoed as he finally reached his father's side. The mercenary pulled his sword out, letting Evans fall back onto the ground at Price's feet. He then turned to walk away, as if he didn't see the young half-elf.

Evans did, though, and tried to reach up to cup his son's face. "My son… you will avenge me," he whispered, and then the ghostly form went limp in Price's arms.

Price felt anger boiling in his blood. He reached for his father's sword, but it was not solid and his hand went through it. All that was left was the wire, but Price knew it wouldn't be a match for a trained warrior. He needed a sword, and there was one place he knew he could find one. Quickly, he made his way back through the battle to his home.

Herrick stirred in his sleep as he heard the distinct sound of metal on leather. Opening his eyes, he saw Price grabbing the sword that Jarak had given him. "What are you doing?" he asked, snapping himself out of his daze.

Price did not answer right away. He looked at Herrick, and his eyes were glazed over as if he was lost in another world. "I need to avenge him," he finally muttered, then turned back to the door and took off running with the sword in his hand.

"Avenge?" Confused, Herrick jumped up and grabbed his other sword from the pile of supplies. "Wait, Price! Avenge who?"

Running after the half-elf, Herrick stopped in the doorway. There was nothing he could see in the streets, and yet Price looked like he was fighting a series of oncoming invisible attackers. For a moment, it seemed to Herrick as if Price and the sword had become one, moving in perfect sync with each other. Swings that would have normally been clumsy by an inexperienced sword handler looked fluid and graceful in the dance-like fight that Price was performing. Yet, Price also fought as if he was in a daze. His eyes glanced around, yet they did not focus on anything… or at least anything that Herrick could see.

"Glorious battle, eh?"

Herrick turned his head, and beside him was a ghost. The face was of a young man from the opening of the helmet, but there were curls of red hair sneaking out. His voice was also very familiar. "Cairan?" Herrick asked.

The ghost of Cairan turned to look back at him, a smile on his lips. "I know you?"

"Yes, but... I know you when you are older than you look now."

"This is a war, boy." Cairan laughed his hearty laugh that Herrick remembered well. "If I live through this, maybe I will look into something for the future. Right now, I look at the present. Are you part of our band, or are you a villager?"

Herrick swallowed, knowing that either choice would be bad. "I'm just passing through, seeing the sights."

"You picked a bad time to travel." Cairan pointed at Herrick's sword. "We could use a good boy like you. Care to join us in our cause? There is a promise of great riches for those that survive. It will set you up for life."

Herrick shook his head and Cairan sighed, putting his hand on Herrick's shoulder. "Suit yourself. I have elves to kill."

With Cairan's touch, Herrick felt his entire body shudder. He closed his eyes for a moment, and when he opened them back up, he could finally see what Price saw. There were mercenaries all over the main street. Some had fallen, their ghostly bodies still, while others were still fought with swords and arrows flying through the moonlight looking for targets to hit.

Price was engaged in a fight with a large man, his

body covered in armor from head to toe. There was a horse nearby, but otherwise there was a wide berth of space around them. Price twisted and turned in the ghostly fight, his dazed eyes locked on the mercenary and nothing else. The movements in which Herrick had seen as a dance now showed to be a graceful set of parries and thrusts in retaliation to the movements of the mercenary he fought. Herrick was amazed since Price had told him that he had never fought with a sword, and Herrick knew the half-elf was outmatched.

Herrick made a move towards Price as to help, but Cairan's hand kept him from moving. "Do not interfere, boy, or else we will have to kill you too. Those who do business with elves have no place in Mora."

Cairan let his threat hang as he stepped into the battle. Herrick kept back, his eyes on the ghostly soldier as he made his way over to where Price was fighting the mercenary. It was already too late when Herrick realized what was going to happen.

"Price!"

Price turned around the sound of his name, and was able to bring his sword to bear as the large warrior came at him, swinging his sword towards his head. The force of the warrior's slash sent the half-elf to the ground.

From the ground, Price looked up at the mercenary and a spike of terror went down his spine. *My gods...I know that face.* Price instantly recognized the young face of Cairan, the man he had helped in the killing of a few days ago.

Death has caught up with me, Price thought as he

attempted to regain his footing. Cairan came at him again, and Price ducked under the sword's arc and then kicked his foot out to hit the ghost in his midriff. Cairan stepped back a few feet, and then came charging again.

There is no skill in his attack, Price noted, just raw anger and bloodlust. He stepped out of Cairan's path, then instantly felt a sharp pain as his arm was scraped by the sword of the other mercenary. For a moment, Price had forgotten about him.

Price jumped back and tried to get some distance between him and the two ghosts. They stood side-by-side as they approached, communicating with nods of their head as they planned their next attack.

It was then that Herrick came to his aid. The man jumped in front of the mercenary that had killed his parents, forcing him to start edging him away from Price. At first, Price wanted to tell Herrick to stop, that it was his fight with the one who killed his parents. However, he realized that he now had Cairan to deal with, and Herrick would not fight the big warrior who had been his friend.

"Die elf," Cairan stated, charging at Price once again.

Price brought his sword up above his head to block the next strike. However, now he wished that he had chosen to take the long way back to the order.

Herrick backed the ghost mercenary away from where Price fought with Cairan. He knew that he needed to make this combat quick, and until then, Price would have to fend for himself.

"What are you doing?" the ghostly mercenary said.

"You are human. The elves are your enemy, not me."

"You attack my friend, you lose the ally status," Herrick said as he swung his sword at the ghost's stomach. The ghost jumped back, then brought his sword around to swing at Herrick's left side. Quickly sidestepping the swing, Herrick brought himself to the right of the ghost and let his sword cut at his rear flank, and he felt the blade slip between the plates of the armor and hit flesh. The ghost cursed out in pain and turned sharply, swinging widely. Herrick ducked the swing and stepped back, examining his sword.

The ghost was bleeding an eerie white blood, yet the sword Herrick held was still clean as it was when he had drawn it. Fire filled the ghost's eyes. "Elf loving bastard. You will pay for this!"

"I've been paying all my life; just add it to the tab." Herrick swung the sword around his head in a warning before he brought it back to a guard position in front of him.

The ghost screamed out and charged again, but this time Herrick was ready. He had been taught that when you brought your opponent to anger, the emotion caused them to loss some of their skill. By staying calm, he would finally get the upper hand over the ghost.

As the mercenary charged, Herrick saw his chance. He brought his sword up and under the chest of the mercenary, aiming to catch him in his ribs, and make a straight cut across his stomach.

The mercenary saw that cut coming, but too late. The sword entered his semi-transparent body, then went straight through it. He collapsed on the ground, holding his stomach in pain.

Herrick pointed the sword at the downed mercenary, who had turned to look up at Herrick. "A curse on your family, for as long as you trust the elves, you are just as bad as they are."

"It isn't what you are that makes you evil." Herrick responded. "It's how you live your life and your choices."

"Believe that and you are a bigger fool that I thought." the mercenary stated, and he started to cough up more of the clear blood. Herrick turned his face away, but he could not help but listen to his dying words.

"You will see that trusting elves only leads the way to pain and death."

Herrick bit his lip. He was about to reply when he heard Price scream out in pain. Price stood a few feet from Cairan, holding his side in pain. Cairan held his sword, the tip now dark red from Price's blood and in a position ready to lash out at the young half-elf again. "You are dead, elf," Cairan stated as he started his swing.

Cairan's sword met another as Herrick placed himself between the red-haired warrior and Price. "Not tonight he isn't."

"Stand down, boy - this is not your fight!" Cairan lowered his sword and stared at Herrick straight in the eye.

"He is my friend."

"One who makes friends with elves dies by elves," Cairan stated. "Save yourself now and let me finish what I started."

Herrick held up his sword in a manner to show that he will defend Price at any cost. "You will have to get through me first."

Herrick was expecting an attack, but it didn't come. No sooner were the words out of his mouth when suddenly Cairan stepped back a few feet and then looked up into the sky. Herrick followed his line of sight and saw that the sun was starting to rise.

Cairan looked at Herrick one more time. "You will regret your choice one day." Cairan said as his image faded away.

Herrick looked all around him. The elves and mercenaries, both standing or on the ground, lifted their heads to the rising sun. Then, one by one, they all faded away, their night of battles finished until the sun set again.

"Herrick..."

Herrick spun around and dropped to Price's side. The half-elf's face was turning white as he trembled in shock and pain. His hands covered his side. Herrick reached down and pulled Price's hands away, then sat back on his heels.

Right below his ribs, a burnt hole was in his tunic. Herrick could smell the burnt flesh and saw no blood. Lifting Price's tunic, Herrick saw that the cut mark was already infected, and the edges of the cut were burnt and crispy.

"What happened?" Herrick asked.

"Sword of...the dead..." Price said, his breaths coming fast. "Oranic..."

"Oranic?"

"Restorative...in my cloak..."

Herrrick reached into the pockets of Price's cloak and pulled out a bunch of tiny bags. "Which one?"

"Start from bottom...knots...sound like syllables..."

Price started to cough, curling up in pain.

Herrick looked at the bags and saw that each one was tied differently. "Damn wizards and their secrets. You can't just use labels, can you?"

Herrick started to look at the knots, and saw one that had three knots in it: one big knot, one small, and another big one. All the others had two or four knots and *Oranic* sounded like it only had three syllables. He put the bag in Price's hands and let him feel the knots. "Is that it?"

Price, through all his pain, let his fingers play over the knots. "No... this is Arsenic. *Oranic*... two knots... small... then big."

Herrick went back to the bags and got the right one, then pulled a little of the crushed leaves out. "What now?"

"Water."

"What water?!" Herrick stood up and looked around, but there was no water in sight. He knew that they didn't have any more in their water-skins either, and from the look of Price's rapidly paling face, trying to find a river was not an option.

Seeing he had no choice, Herrick spit into his hands and then mixed the leaves in with it. The mixture started to burn his hand instantly, and Herrick bit his lip to keep from dropping the mixture. "What now?" Herrick asked, but Price had fainted away.

It's up to you, Herrick thought to himself. He put all the mixture in one hand, then used the other to fully rip away Price's tunic from his wound. Then, turning his eyes away, Herrick placed the mixture over the cut and started to rub it in.

There was a stinking smell, and Herrick could feel

the mixture starting to bubble under his hand. A moment later, a feeling of an electric charge went up his arm and Herrick pulled it away.

The mixture was starting to glow on Price, and his body was jerking a bit in reaction. Price moaned loudly and his back arched painfully a moment, and then went limp on the ground. The mixture bubbled, and then faded away leaving a black scar in its place.

"Price?" Herrick asked, but he did not move or answer. Herrick tried to move the half-elf a bit, hoping that the movement would wake him up, but Price was unconscious. "If you think I'm going to carry your body out of here, you can forget it." Herrick muttered. "Wake up. Price!"

Herrick waited for some time, waiting for any signs of Price waking up, but none came. Herrick sat on the ground next to him and tried to think.

Alright, I'm in the middle of a graveyard town, with no water and a half-elf who is probably dying. What am I supposed to do? Options floated through his mind, and then he remembered the map that Price had drawn for him before they had started.

".. and above the graveyard is the seaside town." Price had said, "You will be able to go there to refresh our supplies, if we need. I am no longer welcome there, though, so I can stay and watch our camp..."

Herrick left Price's side to return to the house and gather the supplies they still had. He wouldn't be able to carry much, so he took what he knew they would need. Walking back, he quickly sheathed his swords and then picked up Price up over his shoulder.

"Just hold on, Price. We've gotten this far, I'm not losing you now."

Chapter 8

It took Herrick almost the whole day to find the path for the eastern town of Elsieke. As the sun was setting, he walked onto the main street, looking for any sign of the local healer. The town seemed small, yet with Price's weight in his arms he felt that the street was going on forever.

Since Herrick knew that Price was not welcome in the town, Herrick had pulled the half-elf's hood far down over his face so no one would be able to see it. He had hidden their packs on the outskirts of the woods, unable to drag them any further. Now, he carried Price almost like a sleeping child.

A passing villager came to his aid, and told Herrick that their healer was towards the outskirts of the town, down by the water and across the street from the local chapel. A twinge of fear ran down Herrick's back, knowing that asking for help was risking both of their lives, but he had no choice.

Biting back any more thoughts of danger, Herrick made his way into the healer's front room. "Hello?"

"What do you want?" a voice behind a curtain

called.

Herrick laid Price on a table. "I have a friend who is injured! He needs your help."

The curtain that separated the two rooms moved aside and an older man appeared. He was in his late fifties with a crown of white hair and deep green eyes. "What happened?"

"We were attacked in the burnt out town west from here," Herrick said, deciding to play dumb. "If you can believe it, we were attacked by ghosts!"

"You were in the graveyard?" the man asked, scorn in his voice. "You must not be from around here. How was your friend hurt?"

Just as Herrick was about to explain what happened, the man pulled back the hood to reveal Price's face. The man jumped back and then looked at Herrick, his face twisted in anger. "How dare you bring this filth in here!"

"What?"

"Do you know who this is?" Herrick shook his head. "This is the young master of the cursed Order. He and his followers have been responsible for the deaths of hundreds of humans!"

"You don't understand, you have to help him," Herrick said. "I need him."

The healer crossed his arms. "I will not heal him. If I did, I would be betraying all those he murdered."

"You're not getting it; I *need* him to help me."

The healer gave Herrick a sidelong glance. "So what, you can go on and cause pain to more innocent lives? I'm calling the guard and they will take care of you."

In an instant, Herrick jumped over Price and the

table and backed the healer into a corner. He brought his arm up to the healer's throat, pinning him to the wall. "Listen to me, old man. I have had more pain in the past few days than most people have in their whole lives. Now, you may not like it, but you are going to heal this man, otherwise you will learn something new about pain."

The two men locked eyes. "Really, what does he mean to you? He will just lead you astray and kill you in your sleep."

"His Order killed the only man I knew that was like a father to me, and they kidnapped the woman I intend to make my wife. They did it against his wishes. Now he's leading me back to her, so we can set this all straight. If you do not heal him, more innocent people will die because there will be no regulation of his Order. Now, do you want *that* on your conscience?"

The old man seemed to consider this for a moment. He then pushed Herrick off him and straightened his shirt. "How much money do you have?"

"Enough," Herrick replied.

"I will take it all, and only then will I heal him."

Herrick let himself consider on how to barter, "Let me keep ten marks for my own food and lodging, and it's a deal."

"All of it and you can stay in my barn - that or no deal. This goes against everything I believe, but I will heal him for your sake... and your money." The old man locked eyes with Herrick, a coldness to them that betrayed any emotion.

"Agreed."

Herrick hated the thought of leaving Price alone with the old man, but it was getting dark and he needed to retrieve their packs. So after handing over his purse to the healer, and giving him threatening looks while resting his hand on his sword, Herrick left.

As he walked through the town, he watched as the people went about their business; parents gathered children from the streets for dinner, and men made their way to the inns for drinks and companionship, many staring back at Herrick in return. Remembering he was a stranger in their town and didn't need any attention drawn to him, Herrick lowered his head and quickly made his way back to the edge of the woods.

Noise from the bushes caught his attention. He stopped, his hand instantly going to the sword at his hip. "Who's there?" Herrick stated.

"Don't hurt! I was only looking!" A small childlike voice replied. A head popped up and smiled at him. "You have some really good food. Did you cook it yourself?"

The small person walked out from behind the bush, holding a bag of dried rations in his hand. He stood about three and a half feet high with a youthful face. His long hair was pulled back in a ponytail that rested on top of his head.

Herrick groaned and released his tight grip on his sword. "Not you again..." he muttered.

"Me again?" the halfling looked around, then back at Herrick. "I know you?"

"Umm...no. No, you don't." Herrick quickly grabbed his bags and took the ration bag back from the smaller man.

"But you must know me!" The halfling bounced in

place. "My name's Gearheart, Gear for short. Certainly that must ring a bell."

Herrick shook his head and turned around to leave. The halfling, Gear, still continued to think, and before Herrick could escape, he heard the halfling bound up beside him. "Wait, didn't I see you in the forest last week?"

"Not that I know of."

"No, I swear, I have your shirt right here!" With that, Gear sat down on the ground and proceeded to flip through the items in his knapsack. Triumphantly, he held a tunic up in the air, its colors resembling that of a work shirt from the Open Trough Inn. Herrick lowered his head in defeat.

"It is you!" Gear shouted and he proceeded to wrap his arms around Herrick's legs. "You saved my life from that wild boar. I owe you my life."

"Oh, it was nothing, really." Herrick tried to pull his legs free.

"No it's the code of my family. I owe you my life, and I can't leave you until I've repaid you."

"No, that's quite alright," Herrick shook his left leg free. "I would have done it for anyone. No need to invoke life debts."

"But I have to!" Gear insisted. "It's tradition. Ever since my great uncle Mubart was in the westward bank and he was saved from goblins by the warrior Tomli. Mubart traveled with Tomli across the continent until they reached the land of Mora. There they got into a great battle and my uncle saved the warrior Tomli when two orcs tried to club him to death."

Herrick held up a hand to stop Gear's story. "I know

the legend of Tomli. There is never a mention of a halfling, let alone a battle with orcs."

"That's because the legends are incomplete." Gear gave Herrick an annoyed look from being interrupted. "As I was saying, my uncle saved Tomli from the orcs, and he repaid his debt then. And he still travelled with Tomli up until he met my aunt and decided to raise his family."

Herrick shook his head. "All in all, you don't have to extend a debt to me, Gearheart. It was just an exchange of services. You got me home, I saved your life. We're even."

"But I..."

"So take care and safe journeys." Herrick trotted away into the forest and in the opposite direction of the village. He heard Gear struggle to pack his things again and follow.

As the trees thickened, Herrick doubled back and hid behind a tree. He stood in the shadows quietly as he watched the red-headed halfling scamper by. He saw Gear look left, then right. After a moment of concentration, the halfling opted for left and continued on. Herrick counted to ten before he moved. He backed away a few steps and then turned... only to find himself on the wrong end of a sword.

"Look what I found, Sirin." A man in simple peasant clothing stated. He had a familiar snarl that show his missing teeth. A few feet away, a balding man turned and Herrick groaned for the second time that night. The man, Sirin, had bruises all over his face, including a fist-shaped one on his temple. "My, my, my... who do we have here, Nacha. I didn't think we'd ever see you again, boy."

Nacha twisted his sword up so the sharp edge rested

on Herrick's chin. The fine line of a wire cut showed across his wrist. "Where's your elven friend?"

"Gone," Herrick replied, his hand resting on his golden sword.

"I don't believe you." Nacha flicked the sword and cut Herrick's chin. Herrick hissed and went to pull out his sword, only to receive a blow to the side of his head. He staggered sideways and felt both his swords taken.

"I told you boy that I was going to keep this," Sirin stated, putting the golden sword into his sword hand.

"Over my dead body," Herrick growled, holding his cheek.

Sirin's eyes sparkled. "That's the plan."

Gearheart took another wrong turn in the forest and pulled at his topknot in frustration. "That human had to go in this direction," he said to himself. Things always made more sense to Gear when he spoke out loud. "I've already gone north and west. And he can't have disappeared. He doesn't look the wizard type. He doesn't even have a robe or anything."

So Gear started to walk eastward this time. The sea was that way, and he knew humans liked living near the sea.

As he came back into a familiar part of the forest once more, he heard voices and the sounds of a fight. Curiosity took over the halfling's mind and he made his way through the brush until he found the noise. Two men stood over a third, one man holding a gold sword at the downed warrior. Gear instantly recognized the downed warrior as Herrick.

"Enjoy your visit with the gods, boy." The bald man stated, raising the golden sword.

Thinking fast, Gear reached into his bag and felt his fingers cover a tiny ball and whistle. He pulled them both out and tossed the ball into the forest beside him while putting the whistle to his lips.

The sounds of twigs breaking made both robbers start. "What was that?" Nacha asked.

"I don't know." Sirin didn't lower the sword and looked over his shoulder.

The movement in the forest sounded again, coming closer this time. It was accompanied by a wail, one that neither man had ever heard before: almost like a large cat shrieking at its prey before it pounced.

"Let's get out of here!" Nacha stated, grabbing the bags that Herrick had been carrying.

"What about the boy?" Sirin asked.

The animal shrieked again. "Leave him for the monsters. It won't follow us then."

Sirin nodded and both men took off running into the forest. Once the sounds of their exit were far off in the distance did Gear step out of his hiding spot. He quickly retrieved his ball, and put both it and his whistle back in his bag before he ran to Herrick's side.

"Wake up!" He shook Herrick, trying to get the human to open his eyes. When he didn't, Gear reached into his bag and pulled out his water-skin and poured some of the water on Herrick's face.

The water made Herrick stir, and he opened his eyes, still dazed from the last blow. He looked around, trying to see where he was, and only found the smiling face of the halfling looking down at him. "…Gearheart?"

The halfling's smile grew. "That's my name. I'm glad you rememebered it. Most people just call me halfling, and that's when they are being polite. Some towns have local names for me that I've never heard of before. Like in Likelrich, they like to call me -"

"Gear." Herrick lifted his hand to his head, trying to keep the pounding from inside from getting any worse.

The halfling, though, kept talking as if he hadn't been interrupted. "And in the forests out near Palleton, they call me 'bait' -" As he talked, he was working with his hands. A cloth came out of one of his pockets, and Gear was mixing some crushed leaves onto it.

"Gear."

"And it was funny because I went fishing with them one day and they gave me a net and told me to go walk into the ocean -"

"Gear!" Herrick shouted, and then instantly he regretted it as he closed his eyes against his throbbing head.

The halfling looked up at him, all smiles. "Yes?"

"What are you doing?"

"Me?" Gear looked down at his hands as he poured some water over the now folded cloth. "Oh, this! It will help you with your cuts."

"Cuts? What cuts?"

"Hold still." Gear came close, and touched the cloth to the larger cut on the young warrior's cheek. Almost instantly, Herrick's eyes flew open and he jumped to his feet.

"Son of a…! What in all the hells is that?"

"Healing herbs," Gear stated, taken aback by the reaction from his companion. He carefully held the cloth out. "It stops the bleeding, disinfects and closes wounds so that they can heal properly."

"Oranic?" Herrick asked as his fingers gingerly brushed along his cheek. The gash, if there had ever been one at all, was gone. All that remained was a tingling sensation.

"How did you know?" The halfling's eyes were now open wide, amazed.

"Lucky guess."

"Well, you must be extreamly lucky. Oranic is very rare and only clerics and wizards know about it. Elves found it hundreds of years ago, but during the wars some humans got their hands on it. Of course, it works differently on humans than it does on elves."

"How differently?"

"Well..." Gear shifted a bit. "It leaves a bright silver-ish scar where the cut was on a human. On the elves, it starts black, but fades away after awhile. The scars don't fade on the humans. But it's very fashionable, I hear."

Herrick looked down at his hands. It had been a day since he had touched the oranic to heal Price, and he remembered that his hands had burned similarly to how his cheek had. There was a large silver circle in the meaty part of his right hand, resembling what had probably once been a sword blister. A few other flecks of silver speckled his hand; probably from tiny cuts and splinters during the previous night's battle.

"Lean down and I'll fix the rest of your cuts" Gear said, refolding the cloth a bit.

"That's quite alright. The rest can heal the normal way." Herrick shook his head and started to look around, hoping that some of his supplies had been left behind. It wasn't long before Herrick realized that everything – including the two swords – were gone. With the sun set, the forest was getting dark fast and Herrick knew there was no way he could go after the thieves in the dark and unarmed. With a sigh, he turned and started back for Elsieke.

"But you're going to wrong way!" Gear stated, trotting alongside of the human. "The bad guys went the other way."

"I'm not going after them."

"But they have your stuff!"

"I'm already chasing after someone and trying to hunt those two will just delay me further." Herrick stopped and closed his eyes, the image of Vesa coming to his mind.

"So where are we going then?"

Herrick opened his eyes and looked down at the halfling. "We?"

"I'm going with you. After all, I still owe you my life, and it seems like you need someone around to help protect you."

"You already saved my life back there. Surely that means that this life debt of yours if paid off now."

Gear considered that for a moment, then shook his head. "I'm a good fighter too. Didn't you say you were hunting someone? It's always good to have another sword." To emphasis his point, he pulled his dagger from his belt. In the hands of the halfling, it looked like a sword.

A small smile came to Herrick's lips. "I can't ask you to come along with me on this, Gear."

"Good thing then that you don't have to ask. Don't worry about me. I can take care of myself, after all." He put his dagger away and smiled. "So, that's settled. Let's go!"

Herrick just hung his head, defeated. "Alright, come on," he sighed, then continued on the path back to Elseike with the halfling bouncing at his heels.

"By the way, I don't think I know your name. After all, you know mine and it's not really polite not to tell someone you are going into battle with your name, and especially if they already know yours. I bet your name is Michael. You look like a Michael. Or Simon… or maybe George…"

Chapter 9

The oil lamps had already been lit by the time Herrick was able to get back to the healer's barn. Gear instantly took in the new surroundings and started making a bed out of hay while Herrick went into the main house to check on Price.

The healer was at the sink, washing his hands. He turned upon hearing Herrick enter and leaned against the counter. "I've done everything I could for him. The rest is up to him now."

"Up to him?"

"He'll live, if he wants to." The healer shrugged, indifferent to the matter. "Now, there is something I was wondering about."

"What's that?"

"His wound was already sealed when you brought him to me, but not cauterized. How is that possible?"

An idea started to form in the warrior's mind as he saw the curiosity from the healer. "Oh, it's a secret. You probably don't want to know the specifics though."

That got the healer's curiosity and he came closer. "Why would you think that?"

"It's a magical herb that elves use."

"Elven magic," the healer growled, shaking his head.

"Just as I figured," Herrick nodded, walking over to where Price lay. He checked to make sure that the half-elf was still breathing. "I mean, who would want to learn the secrets of a people who can live naturally for centuries and never once become ill."

Herrick sneaked a look up at the healer, and from the look on his face, Herrick knew he was debating the idea over in his head. Herrick smiled to himself, knowing that he had the other man hooked. "Well, if you want... no, you wouldn't. Sorry I asked."

"No, what?" the healer walked closer, curious.

"I could sell you some of his stash. He's unconscious, after all. I can tell him that I was so worried about getting him to safety that I must have dropped a few of the herb packets he has. But you wouldn't want them, so forget I mentioned it."

"Wait." The healer put his hand on Herrick's shoulder, keeping him from moving. "We don't have to say its elven magic."

Herrick acted as if he was thinking that over, trying not to laugh to himself. "No... no, you can say you stumbled on them all on your own and discovered it."

"And if you sold it to me, it's not like I did business with the elf."

"Of course not." Herrick shrugged. "So we just need to figure out a fair price."

"You're going to charge me?" The healer crossed his arms. "Let's not forget that I saved the life of that elf, which goes against all my personal ethics."

"Yes, but you took all the money I had for that service, and the night in the barn." Herrick smiled. "That debt is paid. But how about this; give me back my purse, and I will give you the herbs in return. You will make ten times the amount once others hear of your healing magic."

The older man thought on the deal, then nodded and pulled out Herrick's money pouch from his back pocket. "Deal." He tossed the purse to Herrick and then watched carefully as the younger man pulled a knotted pouch from Price's cloak.

"Here you go." Herrick placed the bag in the man's hands. "It's not much, but you only use it a pinch at a time with water on a cloth."

A sneer grew on the healer's face as he pulled away from Herrick to examine the bag. "Now take your elf friend and leave. You can stay in the barn for the night, but be gone before morning or I will call the guard." With that, he took the pouch back into his living space and shut the door.

"Thank you for your hospitality," Herrick muttered to himself as the old man disappeared. He reached down, lifting Price up into his arms and headed for the barn.

Upon entering, the smell of smoke was prominent. Herrick was careful not to drop Price as he tried to run to where Gear was supposed to be. There, he found the cause of the smoky smell.

Gear sat around a small, carefully lit fire. Over it was a spit with a tiny bird of some kind. A basket of bread was next to him, and the halfling absently reached for a roll with one hand while turning the spit with the other. He head Herrick's approach and looked up. "Oh, hi!" He held out the roll to the confused human. "I figured I would get dinner started while you were away."

Herrick just shook his head and carefully lay Price down on a pile of hay. "Where did you get the food?"

Gear looked back at the basket and then shrugged. "I just found them."

"Found them?"

"I'm not really sure. I went for a walk and while I was in the city, I realized I was hungry. And then I figured that you would be hungry, and thought we should have something for dinner. It's not good to go into battle on an empty stomach. And then I realized that I was carrying a basket with food in it, and brought it back so I could make us dinner." The halfling smiled. "There should be enough for all three of us. Who is your friend?"

Herrick sighed as he wrapped the cloak carefully around Price. "He's not my friend. We're working together on a common mission."

"You take care of him like he is a friend."

"I take care of him like he was any other person." Herrick sat back on the ground near the fire, taking that roll and started to eat. "Gear, listen…"

"If you are going to try and talk me out of coming with you again, I will tell you that it won't work. I'm a great tracker. I will hunt you down and find you." Herrick knew it was a threat, but he found it amusing coming from Gear, especially as right after that he handed Herrick a plate with a piece of the bird on it with a smile.

"I was actually going to say that if you are coming with us, you should know what you are getting into."

As they ate their dinner, Herrick told the halfling all

about what had happened at the Open Trough and then the battle in the graveyard town. Gear listened with rapped attention, and he kept giving a look at Price now and then.

"So, when Price is awake, he's going to be leading us back to the forest where this Order lives, and from there, we're going to be going into a battle to save Vesa. There's a very good chance we will probably die, especially now that our weapons are gone." He thought about the sword, cringing at what Jarak would say if he knew that he had let a pair of thieves get the sword from him so easily.

"I may have some friends that can help," Gear offered. "When they left, they were going west. They wouldn't want to go to the ghost town. There is a little village in the woods that I've stayed at many times. It welcomes everyone except humans. The dwarves who live there really hate humans, but the elves try to get them to at least allow humans to pass through unharmed. I can go in and talk with them and see if they saw the humans and where they went."

Herrick reached into his cloak and pulled out the map Price had drawn. "There's not mention of that kind of village here."

Gear leaned over the map, then pointed to a point between where the Order was and Elseike, above the graveyard town. "It's right here. You would have missed it if you went through the graveyard. I guess your friend - I mean, Price - he didn't want you to have to go through a place you weren't wanted."

"That is not why I did not speak of the place," a voice from the hay spoke, and both turned to look at Price, who had turned his head to face them.

Herrick nodded at the half-elf. "Welcome back to the land of the living."

"Hi, I'm Gear. If you're hungry, I can bring you over a plate. There's still some chicken left, and I can boil water quickly to make it into a soup. I know I like soup when I'm not feeling good."

Price gave Herrick a look, and the man just shrugged in return. "Gear owes me a life debt. He's going to help us."

"He will only die if he comes with us."

"If you think you can convince him of that, good luck." Herrick pulled himself up and walked over to look down at the half-elf. "You chose a bad time to get stabbed by a ghost sword."

"I do not believe there is ever a good time." Price reached down to hold his side as he tried to sit up. "Where are we?"

"Elseike."

A look of fear came to Price's face. "I told you we could not come here."

"Yeah, but if you forgot, you were stabbed with a ghost sword and passed out on me. If I hadn't brought you here, you would have died. So I made a deal with the healer, and we have to be gone by sunrise."

"What kind of deal did you make with him?"

"I sold him some of your magical elven healing herbs. He wanted the oranic. I gave him something else with three syllables."

Price's hands instantly went to his cloak, patting down his pockets to see which one was empty. He started to laugh. "You just gave him my bathing soap roots."

Herrick laughed as well. "The guy looked like he needed to take a bath anyway."

"He will know the deception once he tries it out," Price stated. "We should leave now."

Gear looked up, hurt. "But we haven't had dessert yet!"

Herrick closed his eyes. "I'm not asking where you got dessert. But I'm with Price. The sooner we leave, the safer I'll feel. How far is this village from here, Gear?"

"It would be a two days walk."

"We cannot go there." Herrick looked at Price, and the half-elf continued. "I made a promise never to go there."

"As opposed to you just not being wanted, like here."

Gear was looking at the barn door, and there was the sound of voices rising from outside. "Hey guys, I hate to break up your little fight, but we have company coming."

"The back," Herrick stated, helping Price to his feet and putting his arm over his shoulder. "Gear, put out that fire now."

"On it." The halfling started to kick dirt on top of the little fire while he gathered up the rest of the food he had and his bag. Price looked for their packs, then at Herrick.

"We're traveling light. I'll explain later."

The three of them fled the town through the back of the barn, not looking back as the villagers – alerted by the deceived healer – had come to lynch Price and were only left with the empty barn that smelt of fowl and smoke.

Price was not able to travel far with his injuries still healing, so they stopped in the woods near the river, and Gear made another small fire to keep them warm. Price made some tea from his herbs, giving each of them a cup and promising that any aches or pains they felt would be gone by morning if they drank it.

Herrick and Gear took shifts watching the camp, but it was a relatively quiet night. A few beasts howled and tested the parameter of the small camp, but with the river nearby full of fish that were much easier to catch, they didn't come any further than that.

When morning came, Herrick went to the river to get them fish for breakfast. Price had shed his cloak and was cleaning his wounds that had finished healing. Herrick was amazed that the half-elf moved now as if he had not been on the brink of death, and now only just a little sore.

"Those herbs of yours are really powerful," he pointed out as he cleaned the three fish he had caught.

"They do their purpose. That is all I ask of them." Lifting his face to the sun to dry, Price stole a quick look at his companion. "Though I do not understand why you did not just leave me to die."

Herrick did not answer him for a moment before he just shrugged. "I need your help to save Vesa. Anyway, that would have been a horrible death, and no one deserves that. I'd figure you would do the same thing for me."

Price just looked back at the sun, wondering how true that was, and was interrupted by Gear who ran to them excitedly.

"You guys won't believe what I found! I was trying to find some berries to go with our food and there was this path." He waved for Herrick and Price to follow, heading back past camp and into the nearby woods.

The two men exchanged looks, and they both followed, catching up to Gear quickly. It was a five minute walk before Gear motioned for them to be quiet and started to walk very slowly.

There was a small path, and then a clearing with two tents set up. The small fire had burnt out overnight, and the sound of snoring came from one of the tents. What Gear had noticed, however, was the packs that sat near one of the tent, and the weapons that lay across it.

"Travel light?" Price asked as a single eyebrow rose in amusement.

"I said I'd explain later," Herrick answered in a whisper, and the three of them silently made their way into camp. They decided that they would check the contents of their packs later, but at this moment needed to get in and out without disturbing the two men in the tents.

Price and Herrick lifted their packs onto their backs, and then each grabbed a sword. The weight of the golden weapon felt good in his hand, and he motioned for the others to leave. It was then that he noticed Gear had disappeared.

"Gear," he hissed, trying not to raise his voice.

"Over here!" came the reply. Herrick and Price moved in that direction, and then Herrick laughed as he saw Gear feeding a carrot to a pair of horses tied up to a tree just outside of the clearing.

"Looks like we found those horses you've been wanting." Herrick told Price as he walked over to start to untie them, motioning for Price to quickly grab the light saddles that were nearby.

"I've never rode a horse before," Gear said as he went back to pack up the things that were at his feet. Herrick noticed it was mostly food, but some trinkets as well that he was pushing into a bag that wasn't his own.

"You'll get the chance today," Price moved quickly as he saddled the two horses expertly, and then took the lead on one. "Let's get back to our camp and get the rest of our things. They will wake up soon and coming looking for us."

The three of them managed to make it out of the thieves' camp without disturbing the snoring men. When they returned, Herrick cooked the fish for them to eat as they rode while Gear and Price did a quick inventory of their supplies. Within an hour, they were ready with the horses with their packs firmly attached to the saddles.

"We should make that village by sunset now," Herrick stated as he handed out the fish.

"But I told you..."

"Listen, the last time you took us somewhere you thought was safe, you almost died. Gear is welcome there, so he can go and find out if your Order has passed nearby, and help replenish whatever those guys sold of our stuff. I'm sure you need to refill some of your pouches, right?"

Price just stared at Herrick a moment, and then lowered his head in defeat. "I am low on many of the healing herbs now. If this battle takes its toll, we will need them."

"Then it's settled. Gear, you ride with Price. It's time the two of you got to know each other."

"Can I lead the horse?" Gear asked Price, smiling

brightly.

Price gave Herrick a look, and the man shrugged. "You're lighter, he's small; it'll even out the distribution on the horses."

"Can I? Please? I've always wanted to ride a horse and it'll be no fun if I'm sitting behind you. I won't get to see anything except your back the entire way."

"Will you not talk so much if I let you lead after we are on the path to the village?" Price looked down at the halfling, not amused by the childlike personality.

"Sure! I can totally be quiet. You won't even know I'm there."

Herrick just smiled to himself as he left to go put out the fire. A few minutes later, they mounted and led the horses along the riverbank to the village, none of them realizing the welcome that was waiting for them.

Chapter 10

"I really can't take you anywhere, can I?"

Herrick looked over at the half-elf who was tied to the wooden stake in the ground next to him. Price just sighed, looking at the ground and not offering a response, leaving Herrick to stare out at the tiny village set in the woods.

They had found the village easily, and Gear had gone in as planned to get supplies and inquire about if the "large group of scary elves" had passed through this way. Unfortunately, when Gear returned with the news, it was with a small search party lurking in his shadows.

It seemed to them now that one simply does not walk into this particular village and expect not to be seen as suspicious.

During the night, they had been jumped – again – and when Herrick came to he found himself tied to the stake on the edge of the village clearing. His eyes took in the view of straw and wooden homes built in the larger branches of the trees with little bridges connecting them all. There were homes on the ground as well, many with tiny farms that extended well past the tree line.

As the sun started to rise, curious faces started to appear and stare at them. Herrick could see the disdain in their looks; the issues between humans and elves had probably touched the hearts of many people in this village more than others, he mused. But it still didn't explain why Price was tied up next to him.

"Next time we decide to team up, I'm making the battle plans."

There was a small lift to the side of Price's lip. "You were welcome to contribute back then."

"You didn't want to listen to my contributions."

"If we had gotten the horses when I asked, we would have been there by now without any complications."

"So you're blaming the lack of horses for our current problems?"

"I am the one who has been stabbed and nearly died."

"I've been jumped by thieves twice! And right now, I'm the one tied to a stake in a village of elves looking like they are ready to stab me."

Price sighed and lifted his head. "This is just her way of welcoming us."

The way Price said the word *her* had Herrick lifting his eyebrows. He was about to question it when movement in the village caught his eyes and he turned back to see a small group of warriors approaching. There were three elves – two men and one woman – as well as two dwarves and…

"Is that a goblin?" Herrick whispered to Price.

"His name is Salus."

"I thought goblins hated dwarves."

"Not him. He just hates humans."

Herrick looked at the goblin warrior, seeing the deadly look in his eye and took a deep breath. "Great."

"When you both are done talking," the female elf stepped forward, smirking at the two of them. She held a long dagger in one hand, casually slapping the blade into her opposite leather gloved hand. "I believe I have a few questions that demand answering."

"You could have just asked them without the kidnapping and tying up," Herrick pointed out. "We weren't planning on coming into your territory and disturbing the peace."

"No, you just sent your trained halfling in to do that instead."

"He's not my..." Herrick's eyes narrowed, having realized that Gear wasn't tied up near them. "Where is he?"

"We have freed him from your bond so that he can live his life as he chooses."

Herrick laughed. "The only bond I have to him is one he placed on me. You have that story twisted around, lady."

The woman did not look amused now, nor did the rest of her companions, and Herrick let his laughter fade away. "What are you doing in our forest, human, and with such loathsome company at your side?"

Herrick looked over at Price. "She really likes you."

Price just lowered his head, so Herrick turned his attention back to the woman. "First of all, my name is Herrick. What about you?"

"My name is not of your concern. Now answer my question, human."

Sighing, Herrick looked up at the sky to think for a moment before he formed his answer. "We are on the trail of the Order. They raided the town I was in, and kidnapped my friend. I'm trying to get her back."

"The Order does not kidnap humans," the woman stated firmly.

"Well, they did this time, and if I don't find them soon, I'm worried about what they will do to her." He shifted in the ropes, but they didn't budge at all. "Gear suggested that we skirt past your village and he would come in and see if the Order had passed through the area."

The woman shook her head, a sad laugh escaping her throat. "Is this really what the Order has come to, Price?"

Herrick looked between the woman and the half-elf, confused. "So you two *do* know each other?"

Price lifted his head back up, locking the gaze of the woman and ignoring Herrick's look. "Leandra, you know I would never have allowed this to befall the Order."

"And yet it has." The woman, Leandra, walked away from Herrick and stood directly in front of Price. "You swore to me that you would be able to return the Order to its former glory. Was that just another lie you told me?"

"This is Zantos' doing, not mine. I swear to you -"

The leather gloved hand slapped against Price's cheek, the sound of the impact echoing in the village. "How dare you think you can swear anything to me after what you did."

"Oh, I get it... the two of you were together." Herrick chuckled to himself at the realization, but the glare from the male elves made his quiet back down.

"Leandra…"

"No, I told you that the next time we met would be our last, Price. What befalls you and this human will be on your shoulders."

Price just set his jaw. "No, your quarrel is with me. Let Herrick go. He has done nothing wrong."

"He is a human. We do not take lightly to their presence."

"Damnit, Leandra, will you just stop and listen to me?!" Price struggled against the ropes, his voice betraying his emotions. "You brought us here. We were going to leave you in peace. Our presence is not our doing, but your own. Why will you not just speak with me to resolve this, instead of using your village as an excuse to hide the real reason away?"

Leandra had her back turned to Price, but Herrick could see the shift of emotion on her face from his angle. Her warriors saw it as well and looked to her for guidance. She thought for a moment, and then lifted her head towards the trees.

Herrick followed her gaze and saw an old woman in flowing robes standing on the bridge. They didn't talk, but the old woman smiled and nodded, motioning to Price with one graceful hand before pulling that hand to her chest.

Turning, Leandra looked at her warriors. "Release them both. Show the human to where the halfling has set up his camp." She then gave Price a look that could cut him in half. "And you will come with me."

The dwarves stepped forward, axes in their hands. Neither looked happy with the order, but they didn't hesitate to cut the ropes away. Herrick fell to his knees while Price managed to stay knelt upright.

"Are you sure about this?" Herrick asked his companion as he worked to stand back up.

Price nodded. "This is a conversation long overdue. They will not harm you if she wills it so. Just do not leave the camp, and only let Gear talk to the villagers. We can leave when I return."

"Be careful," Herrick said.

Not responding, Price went to follow Leandra as she led him away. Herrick turned to find that the goblin that stood directly behind him. "You will follow Salus. You try to escape, Salus will hunt for you."

Herrick held his hands up. "Don't worry, friend. I don't plan on going anywhere."

"Not friend," Salus grunted and then just turned and walked back towards the village, leaving Herrick to follow in his footsteps.

Chapter 11

Price followed Leandra as she led him away from the center of town and up a rope ladder to a larger dwelling within the trees. She pushed aside the blanket that acted as a door, and he entered before she let it fall to block them from the rest of the world.

It was a modest home; there was a bed of pillows in one corner and a small fire pit in the center that warmed the entire room, a few hand painted pictures on the walls, a small desk with some books and papers, and a basket with clothes. Someone had set up a tea kettle over the fire, and Leandra stripped off her armor before sitting down on a log beside it.

"Why did you have to come this way, Price? I told you I wished to never see you again."

"It was not my intention to come here or to bring you pain, Leandra." Price moved slowly, taking a seat across the fire from her. "It was my companions who choose this route, despite my protests. That does not explain why you felt the need to follow Gear back to our camp and then capture us?"

Leandra looked at the fire a moment, and then

shrugged. "The halfling said that he was in service to the human. He did not appear to be all that bright, and we tried to convince him that he did not have to be of service to anyone."

"Herrick saved Gear's life, and he now feels obligated to a life debt. Both of us have tried since to convince him otherwise, but he is a stubborn one." Price reached over for the kettle, pouring them both some tea, and reaching into his cloak for a particular bag before sprinkling a few of the dried leaves into the water. He handed the cup to Leandra carefully.

"So you travel with this human now?"

"Only until we get back to the hold, at which point I will confront Zantos while he goes to rescue his female."

Leandra took a sip of the tea and then sighed softly. "You still remember how I like my tea. I have not tasted these herbs in years."

"Ever since you prepared it for me like that, it is the only way I drink it."

There was a small smile on her lips, but it quickly faded away. "What has happened to the Order, Price? I've heard whispers of blood and betrayals."

Price stared into his cup. "My father always feared that if the elves from the Order lost the companionship of humans in their lives, they would not understand how to control the emotions that were awakened inside of them. Zantos lost family on the battlefield, just like myself."

"Like many others too," Leandra pointed out.

"But he found solace in anger and revenge. I thought I could help him, but after what happened on the last raid, I know it is impossible. What is worse is that he has brought many of our brothers into his derangement. They are planning a war on the human race."

"This is what you were trying to stop."

Price just nodded sadly. "I failed. And he has cast me out with a death sentence."

"What?"

"If I set foot in the hold, the others have orders to strike me down on sight."

Leandra put her cup down. "Then why go back? You are free of them! You can move on from this."

"Leandra, this is my parent's dream."

"But it does not need to be yours!"

"Yes, it does. If I abandon it, what kind of son would I be to them? I have to fix this."

Lowering her head, she turned away from him to stare at her bed. "We are just having the same argument again."

"Then you know what my answer will always be. I cannot abandon the Order. It is my birthright to lead them; to help them find that harmony we once had." He moved to kneel beside her, placing his hand on top of hers. "If nothing else, I need to stop Zantos before he starts another war. If he does that, no elf in all of Mora will be safe from human wrath."

"Why must it be you?"

"Because it is for ones like me that the Order needs to be there for." His fingers caressed hers gently. "No one else will fight for it."

There was a long silence between them, and then Leandra spoke softly. "I would have, once, before you pushed me away."

"I could not ask you to do that. I still will not."

Leandra turned to him. "Price, you told me you loved me once. Why did that have to change?"

He looked up at her, his eyes betraying the neutral face with sadness and a deep longing of her. "Zantos told me that if I did not send you away, I would destroy you and all that I loved about you. I could never forgive myself if that happened."

"I doubt you would have been able to destroy me," she said with a sad laugh.

Price returned her laughter with a small smile. "I know. But I would not have risked it. Plus..." He smile dropped and he looked at their hands, "...I am certain now that if I had not, Zantos would have had you killed, just so that I would know the pain again and turn me to anger like the rest."

"Is that why you did not tell me why you banished me from the Order?"

"If I had, you would not have gone?"

Leandra looked at their hands for a moment before she turned hers over to hold his. "I cannot forgive you for what you did to me, Price."

"I am not asking for your forgiveness, Leandra."

"Is Zantos really as dangerous as you fear?"

Price just nodded. "He kidnapped the human mate of Herrick's. He wanted me to kill him. When I objected, he struck me and cast me out. He is going mad with his power."

"Then we must stop him."

Leandra stood up, and Price watched in confusion as she strode over to her desk and started to play in a drawer. "Leandra, you cannot do this."

"You said so yourself, Price. If Zantos is allowed to continue on this path, no elf would be safe. That includes those in my village, and I have sworn to protect them." She found a bundle in cloth and turned to face him. "I will not walk away from a threat against them because of a fear of death."

Price walked over to her as she unfolded the fabric. Lying in the cloth was a delicate blood red pendant on a silver chain. The pendant was dull and cold to his eyes, but he knew it instantly. "You still have it."

"You made it for me. But it hasn't sung to me since I walked away from you."

He shook his head. "I cannot ask…"

"Then don't. I will follow you into this battle, Master Price; either at your side, or behind you as a soldier. I think you would prefer it being the first rather than the latter."

He just laughed at that. "You were always the stubborn one."

"You enjoyed that quality in me, if I recall. Now, if I'm to rejoin you to help you with this battle, I will need my magic back. And while you may not wear the amulet on your quest, I know you well enough to know that you would never let Zantos take it from you."

A smirk came to Price's lips, and he reached into his cloak, revealing the identical pendant, only in gold. He carefully put his own on, and then helped Leandra as well. He examined the pendant, and then closed his eyes.

His lips moved as he whispered the ancient magic he had been taught, breaking the spell he had put on her pendant years ago and brought back out the life within it. He could feel the magic inside sing back at him, happy to be free.

"Promise me that you will not use it to destroy me now," he told Leandra as he let go, letting Leandra feel the magic wash back over her.

She smiled at him, and then reached out to touch his arm. Price suddenly felt his entire body stiffen, frozen in place. His eyes darted to stare at her in fear, but she just leaned in and whispered against his lips, "then don't give me another reason to," before she kissed his lips.

His body was released a moment later from the spell, her lips still pressed against his. When they broke apart, he just shook his head at her. "That was cheating."

"I know. And I missed you too."

Price laughed as he pulled her into his arms. He initiating the kiss this time and held her close, swearing to himself that this time, he was never going to let her go.

Herrick sat across from Gear and Salus at the fire pit, listening to the halfling going on and on about an old family story. The goblin was interested actually in hearing the tale, but he kept his eyes on the human, never letting his weapon leave his lap. The story, of course, eventually ended and turned into a question game, Gear wanting to learn all about their new "companion".

"Salus is a friend of the Village of the Forest Spirit," the goblin stated gruffly. "When Salus was born, head was too small for helmet. Arm too weak for club. Clan did not care for Salus. Said Salus would be useless. Salus was taken to mountain and left in hole. No one came back for Salus."

"That's horrible!" Gear handed out bowls of food to Herrick and Salus. The goblin sniffed at the contents, then adjusted the club on his lap so that he could keep the weapon close as he ate from the bowl with his bare hand. "Isn't that horrible, Herrick? No one should be thrown out of their own village, no matter how different you are."

"It is very sad," Herrick nodded in agreement, looking for a fork.

"What does human know of that? Human does not care about the lives of those who are not like themselves. Humans…"

"Just because other humans haven't treated you well, doesn't mean that I will be the same," Herrick pointed out. "Aren't I sitting at this fire with you, sharing a meal?"

"You do not want to be here. Salus keep you here."

"And have I once tried to hurt you, or Gear, or anyone in this village?"

"You are waiting for Salus to lower his guard."

Herrick sighed and was about to respond when Price and Leandra walked into the circle of their firelight. Herrick noticed two things immediately: the first was that Price was not harmed, tied up or being escorted by any of the other guards, and the second was that both of them were wearing the amulets of the Order out in the open.

"I take it the two of you made up."

Price managed a hint of a smile at his human companion. "We have. Leandra has offered to join us. Stopping the Order and their destructive ways will be mutually beneficial to us and to the Village of the Forest Spirits."

"If there is going to be any hope of peace between the humans and elves, it will not exist with the rogue behavior that the Order has become," Leandra added. "We must heal them from their own derangement at the hands of Zantos."

Herrick nodded. "Alright then. I guess the more the merrier."

Gear grinned and held out two more bowls of food to Price and Leandra. "We're going to need more horses. And food! I will have to go and gather some more supplies. Herrick put me in charge of the supplies because I can always find what we need. Are we going to need anything else?"

"Salus can help too." The goblin stood up, hitting his chest armor with one arm. "Salus is good warrior. Salus will help defend Forest of Village Spirit."

Leandra looked at Price a moment. "Salus, perhaps we can use your help. How good of a friend are you to the Goblin King these days?"

"Gobin King does not like Salus. Gobin King think Salus weakling because of size. Salus smaller than all goblins."

"Do you think he would be willing to talk with us, though?"

Herrick held up a hand. "Why would we need to talk to the Gobin King?"

"The goblins have caves in the same mountain that the Order has their new stronghold," Price informed the group. "I know that Zantos has an agreement with the Goblin King to not attack and in return, we would not harm them. And when I say agreement, it was actually a pretty nasty meeting that went between the two. The Goblin King was not happy, but doesn't attack the stronghold because they don't know how to counter the magic."

"But if we could counter their magic…"

"The goblins could swoop in and overtake the stronghold in a matter of minutes."

"Goblin King would be pleased with that. Goblin King would be very happy to spill elf blood and take the stronghold."

Leandra moved closer to Salus. "But would he be willing to help and not kill the elves? Just to capture them, and we would make them leave. Then he can have the stronghold and everything left in it after we get out the human female and some of the Order's artifacts?"

Salus had to think a moment, and then shrugged. "Salus does not know."

"Then we need to have an audience with him. Can you do that for us, Salus?"

The goblin was obviously struggling with the idea, but gave a single nod again. "Salus will go and ask Goblin King to speak with Leandra. Salus cannot promise that Goblin King will agree."

Price placed a hand on the goblin's shoulder. "That is all we can ask of you, Salus. Thank you."

The goblin moved to pull his shoulder away from Price's hand, but stopped and looked at Leandra. The elven woman gave him a smile, and Salus nodded again. "You are welcome. Salus leave now. Salus talk to Goblin King tomorrow. Salus meet you at forest edge when done."

Price let the goblin's shoulder go, then took up the bowl of food Gear had given him and started to stir the meat as the goblin took his leave of the group. "We will need to come up with two plans now," Price told the group. "Depending on if the goblins join us or not, it's not going to be easy to break into the stronghold."

"When has any part of this trip been easy?" Herrick asked. "I noticed that you're offering to give the goblins the stronghold. Don't you need that place for your group once you've broken them from Zantos' influence?"

"I have been thinking on that, and I think that it would be better to abandon it. That was Zantons' home, not ours. I think that if we move back to the graveyard and made it into a village again, it would heal the scars of battle that continue to haunt it."

"So you're going to ask all of them to move to crazy ghost town?" Herrick shook his head. "That's not going to be all that enticing."

"That or they can come here," Leandra said. "We will always welcome those like us who are lost and looking for a place to call home."

"It's very pretty here. I would choose to move here," Gear piped up, not wanting to be left out of the conversation. "There are enough trees for everyone!"

"Just as long as there's no humans in the group, you'll be set." Herrick looked down at his bowl.

Price looked at Herrick a moment. "When did you start to worry about how the rest of my Order would be treated in this?"

"What, the human's not allowed to care about anyone but himself?"

"That is not what I said."

"No, but that's apparently how you all seem to think

I think." He put his bowl down, standing up. "I'm going to take a walk. That is, if your people will allow me to." He looked at Leandra, and the woman just nodded.

Price watched him go, and then sighed. "I do not know what just happened here."

"He feels that you guys are taking over," Gear stated from his spot. "You guys don't seem to remember that they have the woman he loves trapped. You just keep talking about taking down the whole big Order, but not about how to save her." He shrugged a bit, picked up Herrick's bowl to clean it out. "And seeing you two being all hand-holdy and cute together probably isn't helping either."

"He is a very emotional man," Leandra stated as Herrick faded into the shadows. "I never would have taken a human as being such."

"The stories we tell about humans not having compassion are lies," Price said softly as he stood up. "I think they tend to be the most emotional creatures in all of creation and are ruled by their emotions, and not all of them are good. Sometimes I forget that. Excuse me. I believe it is time I tell him things he needs to know."

Price nodded to the group and took his leave, hunting out Herrick in the dark.

Price soon found the man leaning against a tree, looking up at a spot where the tree canopy opened and the starry night was visible to all.

"You know, in any plan that we decide on, my first priority will be to get your woman free," Price said as he went to stand beside Herrick and just looked at the stars. "I swore to you I would help you save her, and I will not go back on that."

Herrick let out a deep breath and turned to face Price. "I just want to know why they took her in the first place. If your kind hates mine so much, what would they gain from having her there? It doesn't add up."

"I do not think you would like the answer I believe it to be."

"Try me."

Price looked at Herrick directly, sympathy in his eyes. He knew what he was going to say would not be taken well. "The Order had always been a coexistence of humans and elves. That trust was broken, but it still the foundation. Zantos and I had been at each other for years now about how we have strayed from that path. I wanted to return the harmony, no matter how broken it was."

"You'd think he would want that."

"You would, but he lost his wife in the battle to a very horrible human man who kidnapped her, ravished her, and then he took her life. Zantos was not in time to save her, and I think that turned him mad."

Herrick felt his jaw clench. "You think he intends to do the same to Vesa? Why didn't you tell me this before?"

"I do not know for sure if this is his plan, but if you had known, it would have just driven you to storm in without a plan or help. He is waiting for both of us, and we have to outthink him. Bring in factors that would disrupt the theatrics he will have set."

"Like the goblins."

Price nodded. "I was going to talk to them myself when we got closer, but Leandra is more of a friend to them than I am. With her on our side, they will surely help us."

"Will Vesa still be alive when we get there?" Herrick was looking back at the stars now, trying not to let Price see the anger and fear that he knew was surging through him.

"She will be. Zantos would want you to witness her death." He thought a moment, and then sighed. "Of course, there is another purpose she could have to him."

Herrick looked back at him. "What?"

"I was the only half human left in the order. We are very rare these days, since most were killed in the war, and the rest went into hiding from the humans. Zantos relied on me to give insight on human emotions and thoughts. Without me in the Order, he would need another to be able to understand their mentality before a battle."

It took a moment, but the meaning of that sunk into Herrick's mind and he shook his head. "I know Vesa. She would rather be killed than be used like that."

"She is a very strong woman, from what I saw of her. There is power in her. She reminds me a lot of Leandra, in fact. If she is as strong as I believe, I am sure she will be alive when we get there. And we will save her, Herrick, or die trying."

"I don't plan on dying anytime soon, you know."

Price smirked and grabbed Herrick's forearm. "Neither do I. We will finish this as we started it, Herrick. No matter what, I will be at your side until the end."

Herrick smirked back, slapping Price's shoulder before they turned and started back for the fire.

"So, Lenadra and you…?"

Price just laughed. "I have been waiting for you to

bring that up. Yes, Leandra and me. She is unlike any other woman I have met, and she captured my heart many years ago."

"So what happened?"

"I told her it would be safer for her not to stay with the Order. I did not want her to be tainted by Zantos' growing madness. When she would not leave on her own, I felt it was necessary to create a reason for her to."

"I bet she loved that."

"That is why I said I would not be welcome here. I am surprised she did not kill me on sight."

Herrick chuckled. "You obviously still have a lot to learn when it comes to women."

"I would not disagree on that. She has confused me on one too many occasions."

They reached the edges of the firelight, and both men stopped to watch Leandra helping Gear clean up the fireside. After a moment, she stopped and looked in their direction and smiled at Price.

"You are very lucky," Herrick told his friend softly. "I would suggest that you do not let her go again."

"I do not plan to."

"You help me get Vesa, and I'll help you secure a future that the two of you can share; that sound fair?"

Price looked up at the human. "That sounds like the best plan of all."

Chapter 12

The four left the Village of the Forest Spirits just after the sun rose, wanting to get to the Goblin King's realm before mid-day. Leandra had found them another horse, as well as a pony for Gear to be able to ride on his own. It would keep them from any further delays on the trip that should have them at the Order's stronghold by nightfall.

As they came out of the forest, the stronghold was finally visible to them. The large mansion seemed to be cut right into the mountain that shot up alone in the large clearing with forest surrounding all the edges of the clearing. The trail leading to it was visible, but the group stayed off it, heading instead to the shadow of the mountain where the goblins lived.

As they got closer, the perpetually dark grottos started to come into view. Herrick smelt the stench first and had to fight to keep his composure from getting sick. Price leaned over, giving him a tightly wound set of herbs.

"Chew on this. The juices it makes will keep you from becoming sick," he said in a whisper. Herrick started to chew on the herbs and felt better immediately as the scents of lavender and mint filled his senses.

"We dismount here," Leandra stated, sliding off her horse. There was a tiny stream that was uphill from the grotto, and she lashed her horse to a bush near it. The others followed suit, and the four of them walked the rest of the way.

Just on the outskirts of the grottos, Salus was waiting. "The Goblin King will speak to Leandra. I will show you the way."

The grottos were lit by torches that lined what were a series of paths through broken wooden shacks and cobblestone caves. Garbage littered the streets, and against the wall there was a large pile of decaying trash that Herrick assumed was year's worth of scraps from meals.

As they walked, goblins of all ages poked their heads out from their buildings and watched them pass. No one made a move to challenge their presence in the grotto, but Herrick could hear them whispering as some of the larger males measured them up with their eyes. *It's probably because their king is allowing us an audience that they haven't attacked*, Herrick thought.

Salus led them through the streets until they came to a halt just in the center of the grotto. There, the group held a collective breath as they viewed a tiny garden paradise in the middle of the filth. Soft grass cushioned their feet again instead of the hard packed earth that made up the grottos, and a soft glowing moss covered the first ten feet of the base of the mountain to keep the darkness back.

Tiny flowers grew within the tall grass that framed a long walkway, and at the end was a wooden archway encased in ivy. A pile of pillows and trinkets were under the large archway, as well as a man. He was reclining on the pillows, sipping from a silver cup as they approached. Herrick could tell that he wasn't a full human from his height and the angular features in his face and body.

"What is he?" Herrick whispered to Price and Salus led Leandra closer to the man.

"He is what they call a hobgoblin. Half man, half goblin. There is a sect of goblin women who are trained on how to seduce a human man to create the next heir. Only male children from these matings are allowed to live, and they can only mate once every six years. When they are eighteen winters old, there is a battle in which the Goblin King battles all the hobgoblins of age, and the one who survives will be the Goblin King for six winters."

"But why not just have a normal goblin rule?"

Price just shrugged, not knowing the answer to that question. Herrick was about to ask another question when laughter filled the air around them and the Goblin King stood up.

"You think that you can defeat the dark elves who live in the mountain? There have been many who have tried. None have ever succeeded. What makes you four different?" His yellow eyes peered out at the group, a wicked smile on his lips.

"That is why we have come to you for help, Goblin King," Leandra stated, her voice calm and almost melodic as she spoke. It was different than before, and Herrick realized that he was drawn to this new tone, just as the Goblin King who turned his attention back to her with an almost fascinated look. "We know you and your people have means of getting into the hold for food. We would like you to show us these ways."

"We can show you these ways, but what is in it for Goblin King?"

Leandra looked back at Price, who just nodded. "If you show us these ways, and your warriors help us disarm the elves, we will make them leave the hold and you can bring your family to live there."

"You would give the mountain castle to goblins?" His voice was tinges with laughter as if he didn't believe it.

"Yes. We would just ask for your goblins not to kill the elves."

The Goblin King waved his hand and leaned back into his cushions. "The elves would kill us without stopping. Why we not do same? We attack and take the mountain castle and kill them all."

"But you haven't yet." Price stepped forward, causing a few of the goblins to hiss at him. "Goblin King, no other army is strong enough to go against them, and your warriors have been helping steal and barter from them for years. That knowledge is power that they will never feel you have because you've never threatened them. You have an advantage."

"Still do not see why we should. If we lose, then the elves kill us."

"If you don't, eventually they will anyway. Do you really think they would have let you live here if they didn't have a plan for you?"

The Goblin King's dark green lips pressed together. He stood and started to pace a bit, his fingers playing with a few rocks until he threw them against the moss covered part of the mountain. "Goblins will get you inside," he decreed. "If we fight, it will be that we can by any means. If an elf goes to kill us, we kill it first. We do not have your freezy magic so we protect ourselves. I will not let goblins die to save elves. Elves will then leave mountain castle and go live in woods."

Leandra put a hand on Price's shoulder. "We can't ask them to just die for us, Price. I want to save them as much as you, but sometimes sacrifices must be made."

"The ones who don't fight won't be killed," Herrick added. "If we can find a way to let them know that, hopefully there will be some who will listen."

Price took a deep breath, and then nodded. "Okay, Goblin King. I will agree to that."

The Goblin King's face lit up and he clapped his hands three times. "It is done. We wait until night, and then we show you way in." He moved past them, heading into the main part of the grotto to start gathering his troops, leaving the group of four behind to start planning their final assault.

There was only one wall that surrounded part of the stronghold that wasn't imbedded into the mountain. The stronghold was simplistic in design, and not intended for a village or markets to exist in its borders. It was a home, and nothing more. The wall, however, was high and the only gate was shut tight with their secondary doors closed and barred as well.

"It is almost as if they know we are coming," Herrick pointed out sarcastically. He stood along the shadows of the wall with Price, Leandra, Gear, and Salus. On the other side of the gate was the Goblin King, dressed in a ridiculous mismatched set of armor, along with at least three dozen goblins. Others had already gone to other parts of the wall to try and breech it.

"I did not doubt Zantos would have expected me to return, or for you to challenge him," Price whispered back. "They will be ready."

"If only we could fly over these gates."

Price looked back at his companion and there was a small smirk on his lips as he rubbed his amulet. "That would be too easy, you know."

Herrick smirked back at his friend. "Just wishful thinking."

Salus motioned with his arm for the group to follow as Alric and his group shifted to reveal a sewer pipe. They had pulled away part of the grate, and warriors were starting to slip through. "Salus will guard from behind. You must get in quickly."

Gear's nose wrinkled. "It smells horrible. Maybe I could stay behind and watch the horses?"

"Gear, you don't have to come with us," Herrick told the halfling. "It's going to be dangerous."

"I'm not afraid of the danger," Gear stated firmly. "I just don't want to walk in sewage. I have standards and walking in sewers is a big no for me."

Herrick smiled, because he could see that the halfling was shaking. Gearhart didn't know how to use any of their weapons, but didn't want to be a disappointment to the rest of them now that the time for the battle had come. Herrick put a firm hand on the shaking shoulder.

"Alright. Make your way back to the horses carefully and make a camp somewhere that you can't be seen. We'll come back in two days."

"Are you sure? I should be here to protect you."

Leandra walked over, leaning down. "I don't trust my horse with just anyone, Gearhart. I expect her to be well fed when I return."

Gear's face lit up a bit. "I will make sure that they are all taken care of."

"We'll see you in two days."

Herrick watched as the halfling started to head back down the mountain the way they had come, and felt a bit of relief knowing that the halfling would be safe. Then Gear's voice called back up the path. "Don't die, Herrick! I don't want to fail on my first life debt because you died before I could save you."

Price's snicker made Herrick roll his eyes before turning to reply, but the halfling was already gone.

Once inside the gates, the time for laughter was gone. The sewer led them to a swamp outside of the main hold that they ran through in pairs to get to the wooden door of what would have been a servants' quarters. When the door wouldn't budge from anyone's efforts to push it, Price walked up to it and closed his eyes.

The amulet was in his left hand now, and he held his right one out in concentration. The amulet glowed, and there was the sound of a large beam of wood cracking before the door burst open. The echoes of fighting came from inside as some of the goblins had already breeched the hold from the other side.

The warriors pressed past them, heading into the direction of the battle with their weapons held high. Herrick started to follow, but Price grabbed his arm. "No, we will find your woman first. Then you two will escape and I will find Zantos."

"Don't even think about it," Herrick warned. "We're in this together. We both find Vesa, and then we all will face your enemy."

Price looked at Herrick a moment, wanting to warn the human that he didn't think he would live through this battle, but he could see the determination in his eyes. "Fine, but we will still get her first. One of the goblins will see to her safety."

"If she doesn't join us instead. Trust me, she can be a beast when she wants to be."

Price nodded down a hallway that Leandra was already guarding with her bow outstretched in front of her. The three of them took off running; Price leading with Leandra at his side, and Herrick bringing up the rear.

They met little resistance getting into the dungoun area of the hold. Herrick assumed that most of the elves were busy upstairs with the goblins, and they only had to deal with the two set up to guard the cell.

Leandra had an arrow aimed at them, and Herrick noticed that the same hand that held the base of the arrow behind her ear also had her pendant wrapped around her fingers. The gem glowed and he could see Leandra's lips moving silently.

Price stood in front of her, his own amulet in his hands as he looked at the guards. "Zantos' time is at an end, my brothers. I have come to free the human, and regain the glory of the Order. You will stand down."

"We cannot do that, Master Price," the taller of the

two elves stated, their own amulets glowing with a dark green and blue tones that lit the shadows. "He will bring death to those who turn from him."

"I offer you freedom from that. We will leave this place and return home where there will only be peace. Please, brothers, I beg you not to fight me and join me instead. I will not ask you to fight, just to stand aside and leave this place forever."

The other elf looked beyond Price at Leandra and gave her a small smile. "I will leave, sister. Lower your bow from my face."

"Not until you are out of my sight, brother. Release your weapons."

The two guards exchanged glances, and then their hands both went up as their lips moved. The arrow flew instantly, shattering the blue amulet as it went through to pierce the heart of the smaller elf.

The green amulet's light grew, and Leandra pushed herself in front of Price, another arrow drawn when there was a faint trace of movement in the air, and the amulet's light died as the elf's head separated from its body.

Herrick stood behind him as the body fell to the ground, and Price set his lips. "You tried, but I wasn't going to give him time to draw more attention."

Price looked at the two bodies and sighed. "No, I know I will not be able to bring everyone back from the darkness." Reaching his hand out, a set of keys lifted from the body of the headless elf and flew into the air. "We will stand guard. You free her and explain what is going on."

Herrick snatched the keys out of the air and turned, opening the door. The cell was dark, with a straw mat on the floor and remnants of some bones from food and cores of apples. There were no windows, yet a tiny trickle of water flowed down the rocky walls like a silent waterfall. Beyond that, however, the cell was empty. "She's not here."

"What do you mean?"

Herrick stepped back out of the cell, looking for any other cells they may have missed, but it was the only door in the hallway. "There are signs that someone was kept in there recently, but no body, and certainly no Vesa."

"Perhaps she escaped?" Leandra spoke. "The last time you saw her was when they left your village. She could have escaped on their journey."

The thought passed through Herrick's mind. Of all the people in the world he had met, Vesa was one of the few he knew could make an attempt. But he had seen the power that these elves weld, and didn't think she was a match for it. More than likely, if she tried to escape...

"She'd probably dead," he said softly, feeling his body get heavy with the anger.

Price walked into the room and touched the walls. "Zantos would not have someone guard an empty cell for no reason. This was done on purpose." He turned back to look at his companions. "This is a trap."

Chapter 13

It only took a moment for Price's words to sink in before Leanda's eyes widened. "The goblins! He is going to kill them first."

"We have to get back up there, then," Herrick urged. "You said it yourself, we can't afford to let this guy win."

Price nodded in agreement, and the group took off running back upstairs. They followed the sounds of battle which led them to one of the great halls. As they ran in, they came to a room filled with chaos. Goblins were climbing over the bodies of their dead companions to get at the circle of elves that held their amulets and shouted commands. Behind them were the bodies of injured or dead brethren of the Order. Above the dead bodies, on a dais with a knife held at Vesa's neck stood Zantos. She didn't attempt to move: a sign that she was frozen again in the elf's magic.

Zantos saw them the moment they entered and laughed. "I was wondering when you would be joining us, young Price. Have you come to witness the deaths you have brought down this day?"

Price stood taller as the fighting instantly stopped. All eyes – elf and goblin - were drawn back to the three at the door. Leandra and Herrick moved to flank the heir of the Order, weapons armed and ready. It was a standstill; everyone waiting to know what the next move would be.

"This is not of my doing, Zantos." Price's voice echoed off the rocky walls as he started to stride forward. He waved his hand towards the Goblin King, who gave a command in the goblin tongue for the warriors to stand down. They slowly slid back into a defensive stance, blocking the elves in where they stood. "This is the result of your madness, teacher. The sorrow for your loss has taken you to extremes, and I refuse to allow you to destroy the ideals of this sacred brotherhood."

"The ideals of this brotherhood died when the humans took the lives of our families." Zantos pressed the knife closer to Vesa's neck, and she gave a soft whimper.

"The Order is a brotherhood dedicated to mending the wounds between the elven and human races. We swore an oath that we would live in harmony with one another. This is not harmony, Zantos. This is death, and nothing more."

Price looked at the rest of the elves who stood and watched as the words were exchanged. "My brothers, this is not who we are. We were angry, yes. We turned to that anger to heal ourselves from what we lived though, but all it has done is turned our anger on new targets. This is not what we intended to become, and not how we want our children to grow. It is upon us to heal the pain we feel and move on. We must remember who we once were."

"So says the man with human blood in his veins.

You are an abomination, child. You walk both worlds and yet no one accepts you."

"I accept him, Zantos," Leandra spoke, lifting her chin. "The Order, the way it used to be, will always be welcome in my village."

"You abandoned the Order, Leandra. You have no floor to speak here."

"She left on my orders," Price spoke over her, getting looks from the others. "I refused to let the one person who I loved become twisted in the anger and lies that you whispered into our ears."

"Yet you walk her into this field of death." Zantos smirked. "And on the side of a human, no less."

"I'm just here to get your ugly hands off my woman," Herrick said with a smirk.

Zantos looked down at Vesa, a hand coming to stroke the hair along her neck. "She is a beautiful find, is she not? There is so much power deep inside of her, waiting to burst out. I can see why you are attached to such a foul mouthed beast of a human."

"That is why you took her?" Price looked at Vesa as well, and the group watched as her hair had started to move on its own; as if a wind was brushing across her face. "You cannot force any creature to learn magic, Zantos, no matter how powerful their gods makes them."

Herrick looked confused, then at Leandra. "I don't get it. What's going on?"

"Your woman is a fire spirit," Leandra stated plainly, then noticed Herrick's confused look. "Did you not know that?"

"No," Herrick's eyes widened. "I mean, she's

volatile, sure, but she's human."

"A fire spirit is a gift that is passed to children from their mothers, no matter the species," Leandra whispered back, her eyes never leaving the man her arrow was aimed at. "Your kind may call them witches but they are not. They are in tune with an element and can call upon it as needed."

Herrick looked back at Vesa. He had seen her hair move on its own sometimes, and she was amazing in the kitchen, but she had never cast any spells to his knowledge. Herrick had seen witches in his travels and knew how they practiced their magic.

"I don't think she knows either," Herrick pointed out. "I would have noticed if she was a witch."

"An untrained fire spirit is a danger, not only to herself but the world around her. When we finish this, you will want to help her find training. It will help her be able to protect herself."

Herrick gave Leandra a smile. She has not said *if* but *when*, and the determination that they would succeed in her mind helped him refocus back on the battle.

Price had not listened to the conversation behind him, instead having focused on Zantos. "Is that what you have planned with her? A child borne from you and a fire spirit will not bring this Order back to its former glory. It will just rain down destruction upon the land under your lies."

Zantos' eyes glittered with his madness. "What else will he do to make his father proud? He will live without the failures of his predecessor."

"The only thing that I have done in my life that

would not make my father proud was that I chose you to be my teacher."

The air hissed and Price moved quickly, pushing Leandra and Herrick to the sides with his magic before he held a hand out to deflect the ball of red energy that had been aimed at his head. It flew up into the ceiling and exploded in sparks, illuminating the pendant that glowed around Price's neck.

Zantos left Vesa on the dais and started to walk down towards Price, his hand glowing. The rest of the elves in the Order made a path for him, a circle forming around them. "Where did you get that? I know I stripped you of it and of your powers."

"You should always check your pockets around me. After all, I am also known as the bastard thief of Elsieke." Price smirked, fingers clasped tightly around his pendant. "And you cannot strip me of a power that originates from inside of me. The amulet just serves to amplify it."

Price turned his hand, focusing on turning the palm up. On the dais, Vesa suddenly took a deep breath, her eyes widening and she reached for her chest. He half-turned to Herrick, but his eyes were watching Zantos. "Go. I have fulfilled my promise to you."

Herrick hesitated, not wanting to move but Leandra had already shifted to take over the full coverage of Price's back. "Thank you." Holding the sword in front of him, he took off around the side of the circle to make his way to Vesa.

"You will not touch the fire spirit!" Zantos twirled and another ball of red energy flung from his hand at Herrick. Price reached out as well, trying to take control of the blast as it sped towards the man.

"Herrick!" Vesa screamed, making the man turn just in time to see the energy. He lifted his sword hand to block his eyes from the light when suddenly the ball splashed against a barrier and dissolved just inches away from his skin.

"Tomli's sword," Leandra whispered as the energy was absorbed into the barrier, making a silvery gleaming of a suit of armor visible just around the edge of Herrick's body. She smiled and looked at Price. "It creates a living suit of armor around the one that wields it. It will protect him from the elven magic." She laughed to herself. "That explains why he's lived so long."

"Remind me to tell Gearhart his life debt has really been paid," Price told her back. "If not for the halfling, that sword would have disappeared from us before we reached you."

"That is impossible!" Zantos fired another bolt of energy, but Herrick let it come this time, only jarred a bit as the bolt hit and flicked across his body, making the armor appear again before becoming invisible.

"I guess you're not as perfect as you thought," Herrick stated, his fingers tightening on the handle of the sword.

"Kill him!" Zantos pointed at Herrick with a long finger.

There was a moment of hesitation where the elves in the room didn't know what to do before few then started to move, stalking towards Herrick and trying to back him in a corner.

"Kill them all! Including the fire spirit."

Price looked over at the Goblin King and he nodded. He let out a sharp order, and the goblins went to Herrick's aid as the elves started to close in on the human.

"The bloodshed today will be on your hands, Zantos," Price stated as he started to mumble a spell.

"We shall see, half-breed. Come try and take back your tarnished title."

Leandra looked at Price, her arrow aimed at Zantos' heart and just waiting for his command, but Price shook his head. "Help Herrick and his woman get out of here safely. Whatever happens now, just know that I have always loved you."

"You will come back to me." She didn't like the sound of his words, but nodded and made her way into battle, her arrows piercing the backs of the elves that stepped into her path to the dais.

The battle with the elves was nothing like the night in the cemetery. The very real bodies were hard to cut through, even if the sword's unnatural blade was sharp enough to slice through anything it was aimed at. But the look in their eyes and the blood that covered the blade and his hands would be a sight Herrick knew he would never forget.

This is what war is like, he realized. For all his travels, he had always managed to avoid any major conflicts that couldn't be resolved with a good fist fight. There was a temptation to lose the contents of his stomach in the midst of all this, but he knew he couldn't.

He needed to get to Vesa.

The goblins jumped in next to him, fighting the

elves that tried to attack form the sides or behind. They fought like a swarm, crawling over the bodies of the dead to take the place of their fallen brothers. Others crawled over the living; yanking back heads of the elves trapped in concentration of their spells and sliced their throats.

The elves that did not want to fight moved away towards the walls, and the goblins would glare at them as if daring them to join the fight before they moved on. The Goblin King was true to his word though, and his goblins would obey him and not harm the elves that wished to be free of the violence.

There was a scream, and Herrick lifted his head to see that some of the elves had focused their attention not on him, but on Vesa. She didn't have anything to defend herself with beyond the wind that was starting to blow at her hair.

"Hey Herrick, could use some help up here!" she cried as an elf approached with a knife.

"I have her," Leandra shouted, and an arrow went flying through the air to embed into the back of the elf. A moment later, Leandra was on the dais with two goblins. "Don't worry, we're going to get you out of here," she told Vesa as the woman tried to get away.

"Why should I trust you?"

"Because I promised your mate that I would help save you." Leandra reached into her boot and pulled out a knife. "Make yourself useful. If you cannot control your wind, you will need to fight the normal way."

Vesa glared at the other woman as she took the knife and immediately stabbed it into the arm of another elf that was charging at her. She then looked at the goblins.

"What about them?"

One of the goblins gave her a bright grin of half rotten teeth. "We are the heroes," he told her before swinging around to bash the head of an elf in with his studded club just before a green ball of energy left his hand.

The wave of elves seemed to never end, but eventually Herrick was at their side and Vesa wrapped her arms around his neck and hugged him tightly. "I thought you would never come."

"I promised that I would take care of you."

"Well, you've done a great job so far." Vesa pulled back, then ducked behind Herrick as another bolt of energy came flying. He turned and slashed the sword in the direction, and the elf's body fell dead to the ground before her energy finished dancing along his invisible shield.

"How are you doing that?" she asked as she pulled away from Herrick.

"I think it's the sword. I'll explain later, right now, we need to get you out of here."

"I'm all for that."

Herrick looked at the goblin on the dais with them. "Tell the Goblin King that it's time to get us out of here."

The goblin nodded and jumped on top of the throne. He hung on, balancing on his feet with toes that clung to the throne while he shouted in the goblin language across the room, moving his arms along with his words. The Goblin King responded and then turned to a goblin behind him who then took off running.

The goblin got off the throne and pushed it over, then waved at the group. "Get down," he grunted. Not wanting to question what the Goblin King was about to do,

Herrick pulled Vesa and Leandra against the back of the large throne and spread out his arms to protect them from the elven magic being thrown at them.

Moments later, a large explosion rocked the room, tossing stone, elf and goblin alike aside. As the smoke cleared, a large hole was in the side of the room, leading straight out into the darkness of night.

"We go," the goblin shouted over the ringing in Herrick's ears. He grabbed Leandra's hand, pulling her towards the hole as Herrick helped Vesa up.

"What about Price?" Herrick shouted.

"He told me I was to get you to safety," Leandra replied, but her eyes were on the dust-filled room. "Price will find us again."

"By all the hells combined, no. I'm not letting him do this alone!" He pushed Vesa into Leandra's arms, and then leaned in to give the redheaded woman a kiss. "Go with Leandra and the goblins. She will get you somewhere safe and I'll be there as soon as I can."

"Herrick -"

He looked at Leandra, and the elf's angry look resolved into determination and she took Vesa's arm. "Come on. If he wants to be a hero, you cannot stop him."

"I can help him though."

"You will distract him if he feels he needs to worry of your safety. He will be safe as long as he holds onto his sword."

"At least that's one thing he is good at," Vesa commented, giving him a final look before heading towards the hole. The goblins were flooding out of the hole, sliding down the rocky surface of the mountain that was leading to the forest below.

Leandra handed Vesa off to the Goblin King, who promised to see that the fire spirit made it safely to the bottom of the mountain. She then turned to the elves that had stopped fighting and were inching towards the back wall.

"My brothers," she spoke loudly, hoping her voice carried. "Zantos' Order will fall tonight. Those who wish to return to the old ways and live in peace can come with me. The Village of the Forest Spirits will welcome you as home. Or you may leave to live your own lives away from here. But the time to escape is now!" She motioned her arms towards the hole, and the elves talked among themselves a moment before at least a dozen started towards her, joining with the goblins on the climb down the mountain to a better life.

Once the elves who wanted to leave were through the hole, Leandra took one last look back through the dusty room. She couldn't make out much on the other side, but the red amulet showed Price's face in the shadows shouting at someone. Part of her wanted to go to him, like Herrick had, and stand by his side. But she had vowed to help get the human woman to safety, and she would keep her promise.

Herrick was nowhere to be seen.

Chapter 14

Price had watched Leandra go to help Herrick and Vesa, and then refocused his attention solely on Zantos. He couldn't afford to divide his attention anymore, and hoped that they would succeed on their mission. But this was his moment now, his chance to save the legacy of the Order that his parents had started.

He could not fail.

"You have been waiting for this moment, haven't you?" Zantos gripped his pendant tightly, the red glow distorting the color of his hand. "All this time, you were plotting against me. You never understood what we were doing."

"You were after revenge, Zantos. Anyone could see that. I just turned a blind eye in hopes one day you would find healing and come back." Price just stood calmly, one hand on the pendant, the other slightly raised and waiting. "But like a wound, you have festered. I would offer you a chance to change, but I know it is not possible. The infection has reached your heart."

"Is that so? You really think that I am beyond saving?" Zantos was mocking Price as he walked around the edge of the circle of elves that trapped them in.

Price followed his with his eyes. "You will not listen to reason, and you have sentenced the members of this Order to death just to continue on a path of vengeance. You are the reason that humans fear the elves. If there is any chance to save my parent's Order…"

"You will cut off the infected piece before it kills the whole. How very touching." Zantos stood in front of Price, glaring down at him. "Your father was a fool, Price, and your mother was weak for loving him. The ideals you hold onto are their selfish attempts to live a life of abomination."

Price's jaw tightened and his amulet started to glow as the magic stirred in him. Zantos saw that and laughed, and Price just took a deep, calming breath. "Is that all you have, Zantos? There was a children's rhyme once – sticks and stones…"

The older elf's eyes narrowed and red energy came at Price like lightning. He put his hand up to stop it, straining against the power. The lightning, however, didn't dissipate into the ceiling this time as Zantos twisted his hand to wrap the energy around and it struck at Price from behind. He wasn't able to defend from both sides, and it struck him in his stomach, throwing him right at Zantos' feet.

Zantos grabbed Price by his hair and pulled him up, snatching the amulet from around his neck. He dropped it to the floor, locking his victorious eyes with Price as he lifted his boot to crush it –

The wall exploded at that moment, tossing everyone to the floor with the energy of the blast. Price coughed painfully, his lungs filled with the flying dust and still hurting from the lightning attack. He reached a hand out, silently whispering for the amulet to come back to him. The red jewel slipped back into his hand, untouched from the debris that rained down on them.

The explosion had extinguished all the lamps, plunging the room into darkness except for what moonlight was filtering through the dust. Price forced himself to his feet, holding the amulet out and letting the glow light the room around him. "This ends now, Zantos!" he shouted, knowing that he couldn't hold off another attack like that from his teacher.

There was a shuffling sound around him, barely audible above the ringing in his ears. Then, a wind came, blowing the dust away to reveal Zantos standing on top of a chunk of the wall, his arms outreached. His pendant glowed around him, bathing the area in red. From around the room, the amulets of the fallen Order came towards Zantos, their chains wrapping around his arms until there were at least two dozen glowing jewels.

"How are you controlling them?" Price asked, taking a step back. "Only the ones whose energy went into them can wield their power!"

"Then it is a good thing I pushed my power into every amulet in the Order when I took over!" Zantos laughed, his fingers reaching towards Price. The necklace pulled away and then snapped from around his neck and Price watched as his own amulet raced towards Zantos' waiting hand.

"And now, Price ord'Vanele, you will join your parents in death."

Price watched as all the amulets glowed, their combined energy flowing across Zantos' body and through his arm. The energy hit Price's amulet and glowed a brilliant orange before exploding across the room at the half-elf who knew he could not defend himself from it.

The seering pain did not hit him, though. Instead, there was a cry from a human, and Price opened his eyes to see Herrick in front of him. His feet were spread apart, the sword in front of him. Tomli's sword glowed with its magic, wrapping Herrick in his ghostly armor that was absorbing the elven magic but at a cost. Price could see Herrick's clothing starting to burn away, his exposed skin turning red.

"Run, Price," Herrick gritted through teeth, looking over his shoulder at his friend. "Tell Vesa I love her."

"No, you will tell her yourself." Price closed his eyes, praying to his ancestors to help him as he put his arm on Herrick's shoulder. "You were right. We will end this together."

Voices whispered into Price's mind as his ancestors answered him, guiding Price's hand along Herrick's arm until it wrapped around the handle as well. "This is going to hurt," he confided to his friend, a small smile on his lips.

Herrick managed to laugh, his face starting to blister. "Now you tell me."

They nodded to each other in silent agreement, and then Price focused on Zantos and started to whisper an ancient spell. He could hear his mother's voice, guiding him along the words while his father whispered for him to be brave.

He stopped the words a moment as he looked at

Zantos, the elf gone mad with the energy he was wielding and unable to stop as it flowed through him. "May the spirits show you the peace in the afterworld that you would never find on earth," he whispered, and then closed his eyes.

The energy that had been dissipating on the armor started to flow towards where the two hands held the sword. Herrick screamed in pain as he felt all the energy envelop his arm, then hand, burning away at the flesh, then muscle and bone.

"Hold on, my friend," Price said, pressing his body against Herrick as he lifted the sword to point at Zantos. The energy gathered, Price said the final part of his spell.

The gathered energy that had been collected in the armor flowed along the sword until the blade tip was glowing with a pure, white light. It then exploded out, piercing Zantos straight through the heart. His eyes widened in disbelief, and watched as Price continued to funnel the energy, using the armor of his friend to convert the dark energy into light energy, and overtake the darkness within the elf.

A moment later it was over, and Zantos fell to the ground. He was dead, burned from the inside. The amulets smashed to the ground, dozens of jewels breaking as his life energy bled out onto the ground.

Herrick also collapsed back into Price's arms, and they both fell to the ground. Price breathed deeply, feeling the last of the magic escaping his hand that gripped the handle of the sword. A moment later, he realized that his was the only hand that gripped it.

Pushing to his knees, Price looked down at his

human friend and his eyes quickly dropped away from the sight before him. "Hold on," he whispered as he reached for his robe and the packets of herbs.

Price just hoped that he wasn't too late.

Chapter 15

Gearhart had been waiting whit the horses when Vesa and Leandra arrived. They waited three more days with the goblins, but Price and Herrick did not return to the goblin camp. Leandra wanted to go back up to find them, but the Goblin King told her that most of the castle had fallen from the explosion.

"It not safe for you," he said, holding her arm. "Now my home. I fix it. Salus stay here with me. We find them and he carry them to you."

It wasn't the words Leandra had wanted to hear, but she knew that it was true. It had been the risk they all understood going into this, but it didn't make it hurt any less.

"Come on," she told Vesa and Gear softly after the third night. "Let us go back to my village. There is nothing more we can do here."

And they left, leading the group of fourteen elves with them, all somber in knowing just how deep the price had been for their freedom.

Two weeks later, an elf named Solara ord'Nel was

working with Vesa to learn to control her powers. They were on the outskirts of the Village of the Forest Spirits, as Vesa could not find it in her heart to return to Barden alone just yet. This training gave her something different to focus on when her heart was trying not to break at the loss of her love. She was determined to understand this gift now, if only to be able to use it to take care of her village when she finally was able to return on her own.

The morning was foggy, and Solara waved her arm, making the flames from a torch dance and then form into tiny shapes in the air. "Now you try," she whispered softly, lifting Vesa's hand to the flame

The woman tried to relax and focus as the elf had shown her, trying to make the flame move at her will. At best, though, she was only able to make a wind tunnel that extinguished it. Opening her eyes, though, she gasped at the sight that the clear vision revealed with her wind having pushed the fog away.

Three figured were walking towards the village. One was the goblin, Salus, his gait still hobbling from the leg injury he had received in the battle. Two cloaked figures walked on either side, hoods over their faces to hide them from view.

But the sword that revealed itself with one of the taller man's steps made Vesa gasp. "Herrick."

Solara looked as well, and then smiled. "I will tell Leandra," she said quickly, then took off running into the village as Vesa started to run towards the men.

The sound of her approach made Herrick look up, and he had a moment to steady himself before Vesa's arms were wrapped around him, holding him close as she buried her face into his chest. "I thought you were dead," she cried.

"Come on, you know I'm too stubborn to just die on you," he said, his voice a bit gravely. He wrapped one arm around her, pulling her closer to him as he lowered his head to rest on top of hers.

Vesa just laughed, and then looked up at him. Her fingers reached up to push back his hood, intending to kiss him. But she stopped as the sunlight revealed the changed face of the man before her.

Herrick's skin was still red, but healing from the burns the energy had given him. His hair had been shaven off, most of it having been burnt away to lead to a fuzzy set of new growth coming in on the scalp. Instead of the dark color, the new hair was whiteish-blonde in color. Part of his ear and jaw were silver as well, soft scars to cover up the worse of the damage.

He gave her a soft smile as her fingers traced them, then along his neck to his shoulder. It was then where she noticed the robe dropped off. She gasped looking at him in confusion.

"It was a small sacrifice," he explained, his only arm still wrapped around her and squeezed her softly. "You're safe. That's all that matters to me."

"Price!" Leandra's voice echoed through the trees and the other robed figure was tackled to the ground an instant later. The robe's hood flew back to reveal the half-elf, grinning smugly at the woman who straddled him, pressing his shoulders into the ground. "We thought you both were dead."

"It was almost a possibility. But we decided that it

was better not to take that trip just yet." Leandra shook her head, and then leaned down to kiss him hard.

Herrick just laughed, looking at the village. "I hope we haven't missed breakfast yet. I'm starving."

As they ate breakfast, Herrick and Price told their tale about what had happened after the rest had fled. Price had figured out that with Zantos channeling the magic through Price's own pendant, he would have been able to control the energy as well.

The sword of Tomli was an artifact that, as elven legends went, was used to absorb the elven magic. With his own magic absorbed, Price found he could channel the cleansed magic back out through the sword to defeat the darkness.

"Now, mind you, when he told me that it was going to hurt, he really could have pointed out what was going to happen," Herrick joked during the story, his robe still on and draped over his right side.

"It did hurt, did it not?" Price gave his friend a smirk.

Herrick rolled his eyes, and Price continued. He explained about how he used the oranic to seal up the shoulder before he bled to death, as well as the burns that had covered his body. For three days Price tended to Herrick, finding more supplies in the keeps of the stronghold as well as food to keep them going as the stone castle threatened to cave in on them many times.

It wasn't until the Goblin King sent a team of goblins up to inspect their new home that Price had enough help to carry Herrick back down the mountain. Another week of constant applications of the herbs finally made it so that Herrick was able to walk again without pain. A good portion of his chest would forever be a silver flesh, but the rest of the burns would fade like really bad sunburn.

Salus had offered to run and get the women after they had been found, but it had been Price who told him to wait. "You had already thought us lost. I did not see the need to make you worry of Herrick's health when you discovered us alive."

"We knew that we would see you again," Herrick pointed out. "We wanted to make sure that it would only be a happy reunion."

"Well, I never thought you were dead at all," Gear spoke up as he refilling Herrick's bowl. "I told them both that you promised you wouldn't die. Even if Leandra said that I paid off my debt, I told them both that I won't believe it until I see it."

Herrick laughed. "Gear, you're the one who saved us all. If I didn't have that sword again, we'd all be dead, and Zantos would still be trying to destroy the human race." He put down his spoon and put his hand on Gear's shoulder. "Thank you, Gearhart. I will always be in your debt, my friend."

"Same here," Price added. "It is often said that the small actions of one can bring down an empire. In this instance, it was you."

Gear just blushed. "Well, my uncle always did say that I would never amount to anything back home. Maybe he knew I was supposed to find you when I did. Or else he just figured I would get myself killed. I'm glad it was the first one."

Vesa refilled the drinks around the fire, holding the cup up for Herrick to take a long sip. "So what happens now?"

Price looked at Leandra, then Herrick, and then just shrugged. "Now we rebuild our lives. The war is over. I plan to return to the graveyard and rebuild the Order. The ghosts of my parents will not rest fully until peace has been restored."

"Are you sure that's really safe?" Herrick asked. "Won't the battles continue at night?"

"I know a purification spell," Leandra states. "We will put the souls to rest so they no longer live out that horrible night of pain. The life that starts anew on top of the ashes will continue to bring peace to those who died there."

Herrick looked down at Vesa. "What about you, my fire spirit?"

She laughed in return. "I'm about as useful of a fire spirit as a light breeze is."

"You will learn control in time," Leandra smiled. "It took me ten years to be able to master a single spell. Your village is not far from the graveyard, right?"

"A few days walk at most, probably a day on horseback." Price and Herrick nodded in agreement of the distance.

"We will just check in from time to time, and see how you two are doing."

"My inn will always be open to you both," Vesa stated.

"Though you are probably going to need a new kitchen boy." Herrick shrugged his one shoulder. "I think I'm going to have to retire from that."

"That's fine. You can sit by the fire from now on and tell your stories to the villagers… and our children."

Herrick's eyes widened. "Children?"

"If we are going to be husband and wife, I plan on being a mother as well. Unless the battle hurt you in other places you're not telling me."

Laughter filled the air as Herrick managed to turn redder. "No, I'm perfectly fine in that way, thank you."

"Then don't worry about our children just yet," she said, kissing him softly on the lips. "We have all the time in the world now." She settled down, and then looked at Gear. "And besides, I think Gearhart would be willing to step into your apron, so to speak."

"Me?" Gear's head tilted. "You want me to stay with you?"

"Of course we do. No hero should be left on his own." Vesa smiled. "You helped save my life, so you're family now. Will you come back with us, and help me run the inn?"

"Sure! I can totally do that. I can even help cook and teach you some of my recipes. I can make a great boar stew…"

That night, Herrick stood on one of the bridges between the trees, looking out over the forest while Vesa slept. The stars shone brightly, and he watched a few of them streak across the sky. It wasn't long until Price was next to him, watching as well in silent thought.

"I didn't realize you had your own version of the legend of Tomli." Herrick said, looking at his friend.

"That we do," Price replied, his eyes not moving

from the stars. "He died trying to end the evil of a demon that feasted on the anger of others. Our people say he was a gypsy, who had everything his heart could want, and yet left his family and all his worldly goods behind in search for meaning."

"Tomli did have a family when he left. In all the villages and cities I have traveled to, not one has ever remembered that fact."

Price nodded, looking at the sword that rested on his friend's hip. "Will you tell her one day?"

Herrick chuckled, turning to face the half-elf. "Tell her what? That this all started when she chose to love a vagabond gypsy who refused to believe his own heritage and walked right into the same destiny his great-grandfather walked?"

"Not many people know the secrets of the sword," Price pointed out. "But my great grandfather forged that weapon. I had planned on stealing it from you when this was over too, back when we first started."

"I'm glad you decided against that. How did you know then who I was?"

"The weapons magic was made with the spirit of Tomli inside. No one else but an heir would have been able to don the ghost armor. It's the same process used to form the amulets." Price reached into his robe and pulled out the red jewel. It was still in one piece, but cracks now broke across the once smooth surface.

"I wonder if they both knew what would come one day: to know their heirs would team up to save the world from a man driven mad from grief and anger."

"Perhaps. Or it could have been a power greater

than that. After all, we did not just team up willingly, if I recall correctly."

Herrick laughed. "No, in fact I was pretty sure I was going to stab you with the sword after I found Vesa."

"I am glad you decided against that, as well," Price joined in the laughter.

Their laughter faded into silence again, the stars just winking down at the two heroes. Finally, Price took a deep breath. "If you are ever in need, Herrick, I will be there for you."

"Same here, Price." Herrick put his hand on Price's shoulder. "I'll always be in your debt as well."

"There is no debt between us," Price pointed out. "We both fulfilled our promises to one another, and together saved each other's lives."

"Yes, but you did do me one big favor."

"What is that?"

"Tomli died from his injuries after his battle with the demon: bled out right in front of everyone. At least this time, someone at least knew how to stop that from happening. I'd have hated to go out that way."

"It was the least I could do, after you saved my life at the graveyard. The debt is paid."

"In my world, when two men shed blood for each other, they become brothers." Herrick gave Price a quick look, and then nodded. "You're more stuck up than I would normally tolerate, but I'd be honored to be your brother."

"And you are a little more brutish than I would like, but I would be honored as well."

They shook hands, and then smiled in a silent understanding that while their quest was over, it was only just the beginning. There was still a lot of work to do to bring understanding back to the land of Mora between the humans and the elves. It may not happen in their lifetime, but even if it came down to the actions of their own great-grandchildren, there would one day be peace again.

34722245R00089

Made in the USA
San Bernardino, CA
05 June 2016